MURDERS OF CONSEQUENCE
by Ian D Wright

Acknowledgements

My thanks to Sheilah for all her help, ideas and hours of proof reading and editing. Without her hard work, this book would never have been finished.

Thanks also to Ben and Emma for their encouragement and help with the book and the cover.

Setting the Scene

The 60s was a time of great change in the UK, with young people enjoying a freedom that had not been possible before. Work was more plentiful for both young men, and young women and the money earned was spent on buying clothes, cars, scooters, alcohol and eventually drugs. It was the first time in history that young people had fashions of their own.

This story is set in Peterborough, UK in the early 1960s, but deals in incidents that go back to 1935. It also covers happenings in many towns and villages in the Cambridgeshire and Norfolk fens and on the North West Norfolk coast.

In the 60s Peterborough was both a busy market town and a centre for engineering. It still had a cattle market twice a week, where everything from a bull to a bantam could be bought and sold. Although not more than 400 yards from the cattle market, engineers were designing and producing high-tech diesel engines.

The railways had brought prosperity to Peterborough in the mid-1800s and now provide high-speed rail links to London and the North of England. The town had grown rapidly from the time the railway arrived, and as a result, the local population had been enhanced by many people coming to work in the city from London, the North of England, East Anglia, and the Midlands, as well as Poland, Italy and numerous other European countries.

The City stands on the edge of the rich farmlands of the fens and in those days its impressive Cathedral could be seen from many miles away.

This story is a work of fiction. Names, characters and the story are the products of the author's imagination. Any resemblance to actual persons, living or dead, or actual events is purely coincidental. However, all the place names are real, as are landmarks, street names and some businesses, which no longer exist today.

CHAPTER 1

September 1946

George and Mary Kisby were still nervous about taking Gracie, their little Jack Russell, past the POW camp and onto the beach at Snettisham. The war had been over for nearly two years now, and at last, their lives were getting back to a kind of normality. They could not be certain, but they thought that most of the German air force prisoners had been repatriated and they could resume their pre-war custom of walking Gracie along the beach.

Snettisham had always been home for George and Mary. It is a village in north west Norfolk, situated on the east bank of the Wash, the huge estuary that takes the water from four rivers and feeds it into the North Sea. It is a fifteen-mile-wide estuary of mud-flats, basking seals, bird sanctuaries and nature trails.

During the war, the whole area around the beach had been off limits to the people who lived in Snettisham. The beach is almost two miles from the village, except for a few cottages positioned haphazardly along the Beach Road. Before the war, these were considered to be very desirable homes, located as they were, so close to the beach.

When the war started, things changed rapidly. All villagers were kept well away from the military activity that took place on the dunes and meadows just behind the beach. It was where allied servicemen built their skills with guns, hand grenades, mines, bombs, and many other tools of war. The noise was incessant, often throughout the day and night.

It was a war that affected people everywhere, and many lives were disrupted, including George and Mary's dog walking.

Once the war was over, everything had to be cleared up, and the job of removing the ammunition that had failed to explode would be going on for many years it seemed.

Until the POW camp had been erected towards the end of the war, the concerns of the population in Snettisham, were the same as any village in the country. There was the possibility of losing the war and invasion, problems of making the meagre rations go round and the remote but real possibility of having a stray bomb dropped on the village.

But the sudden arrival of a large group of Germans in the village made George and Mary extra nervous. When the Germans walked past the Kisby cottage, George and Mary would scuttle inside, lock the doors, and close the curtains. George always thought the Germans looked too cheerful. All the photographs in the newspapers showed them looking stern and quite frightening. But when you met POWs in ones and twos on the street they would smile and say hello. They must be up to something, George thought, and he was going to keep well away from them.

As they passed the camp and reached the edge of the pebble beach, a door of one of the huts in the camp opened, and they saw a man standing in the doorway. He walked a few steps and emptied something into a dustbin. Someone inside the hut said something to him. He gave a deep guttural laugh and went back inside. So there were still some of them here.

They paused and considered for a few moments if they should go on or turn back. At that moment, Gracie suddenly scurried off. Normally she never strayed from their sides. But something had attracted her, and she was already a hundred yards ahead of them and not slowing down. Then she began to bark.

George and Mary were frantically calling her name, but she took no notice of them. It was most unusual. She was such a well-behaved dog and saw her role in life to protect her owners. But not today. She had stopped and was now barking excitedly. With each bark, she leapt several inches into the air as if emphasising the importance of her find.

Walking quickly on a pebble beach is not easy, especially when you are in your sixties. The Kisby's were both breathing heavily as they approached Gracie. George's eyesight was better than Mary's and as he struggled along on the loose, rounded pebbles, he could suddenly see a long, dark object lying in the shallow surf.

It looked like a dead seal. There were many of them in the Wash, and it was not unusual to see them stranded on the beaches.

'It's alright Gracie. It's nothing. Come here. Good girl.' George shouted over the sound of the surf moving the pebbles.

But Gracie was not open to persuasion. She continued her frantic barking and jumping. It was late afternoon now, and there was a cold breeze blowing across the water that George hadn't noticed when they were behind the sand dunes. But he was hot from his exertions, and he was glad of the breeze.

He was nearing the frantic dog now, and she was beginning to calm down.

Mary was also reaching the scene when she heard George call out.

'Bloody hell!' he shouted. Mary stopped in surprise. George was not a man to use bad language unnecessarily.

'What is it?' she asked, managing to keep her voice calm because she knew it had to be something very strange to make George swear.

'Bloody hell' he said again, this time quietly as if he was talking to himself. 'It's a body. A man's body. Stay where you are Mary. Stay where you are.'

Gracie seemed to sense that the mood had changed and her excitement subsided to a few disgruntled growls at the object lying in the surf.

The dog walked back to where Mary stood in shocked silence.

'What should we do?' Mary said in almost a whisper.

'Go back home, and I'll ring the police from the kiosk at the end of the road.'

'Won't it get washed away?'

'No, the tide's coming in. It will just get pushed higher up the beach.'

Mary looked doubtful, but she was not going to argue. She wanted to get home, and they still had to make their way passed the POW camp.

George made his call to the police, who were at first rather disbelieving of his story and, in fact, George was as well. It seemed unbelievable, and he began to wonder if he had dreamt the whole thing. But then, looking through the dirty glass of the telephone kiosk at Mary's shocked face, he pulled himself together and began to speak with more certainty.

It was a busy time for the police in the UK, with several thousand POWs being repatriated and hundreds of thousands of British troops returning home. People coming home to families they have lived apart from for years, relationships to rebuild, wives who welcomed their returning heroes and other wives who had enjoyed a better life without them.

The officer George was talking to kept having to answer questions from other people in the room with him as well as dealing with George. He was beginning to think he should have left it until the next morning when he would perhaps get more of their attention. But after several attempts, he managed to tell the story.

They said that he should go home and they would come to his house and collect him. Then he could show them where the body was. He gave them his address, explaining that their cottage was on Beach Road, so they were easy to find. He was about to ring off when the officer said it was likely to be an hour or so. George asked him if he thought there might be time for him and Mary to get their dinner. He waited for a reply, but all he heard was the click of the line going dead.

George told Mary that she had better wait until he got back before putting dinner on the stove. He sat in the armchair facing the front window, craning his neck to see when the police arrived. He was anxious not to keep them waiting. Eventually, he just had to stand up. His neck was beginning to ache, and his stomach was reminding him that lunch was six hours ago. It was completely dark now, and he had to peer close to the net curtains to see anything on the street outside.

Situated only a few miles from the Royal estate at Sandringham, Snettisham was quite a large village. A few miles further away from the historic town of King's Lynn where the largest police station in the region was located. The hard-pressed police force was thin on the ground and meant that there was no Bobby in the village in the evening and overnight. In any case, he could not have dealt with an emergency of this scale, George thought to himself. So, he would just have to wait for them to come from King's Lynn.

Cars were few and far between in the village before the war, and petrol rationing had reduced their use even further. George knew that he would easily see a car arrive, but he just could not sit still. So, he stood and looked through the net curtains. Mary sighed heavily and took her knitting out. The click of the needles somehow felt very calming to George, and he sat down.

Mary smiled and said, 'They will be here soon. You'll see.' And they were, an hour and a half later.

George pulled his winter coat on; the one he used for funerals and weddings. He had not used it often since the war started. Mary didn't like going out these days. The start of the war had turned their comfortable retirement upside down, and now at the end of it, the turmoil was continuing.

The police arrived in a car and van. They parked outside and waited for George to show himself. As he walked out of the front door, the back door of the police car opened and George climbed in. There were already four very large policemen in the car, so he squeezed into the space that was left, sitting at an angle, one bottom cheek on the seat, the other on the rear wheel arch.

The bulky figure on the front passenger seat spoke, without turning around. 'Sorry we're late Mr Kisby, but we had a few problems getting everything together. It's a difficult time of night for us. Shift changeover and shortage of staff. We go down to the POW camp, right?' The voice was loud and deep, with a strong Norfolk accent. George felt reassured.

'Yes, we were walking our dog. It's really shaken my wife. I don't want to be away too long, or she will start to worry.'

The figure in the front seat made a great effort to turn in his seat and look at George. 'As soon as we find what we have come for I will arrange for you to be taken back home.' Mary's wonderful stew, thought George. That's something to look forward to.

'Thank you, Sergeant,' he said, having seen the stripes on the policeman's arm. 'It's going to be cold on the beach.'

They parked the two vehicles just passed the POW camp gate. The five men in the car and two others from the van assembled in a ragged circle to hear the Sergeant's orders.

He stood in the centre of the circle, which was illuminated by the headlights of the car. George could see that he was a big, broad-shouldered man. He quickly organised the group into a line across the beach. The policemen moved slowly forward, each with a torch lighting the area ahead.

George and the Sergeant moved slowly behind the line. It was a bleak and eerie sight. A bitter wind had replaced the cool breeze of the afternoon, and with darkness, it had taken on a feel of winter. The boots of the searchers crunched on the loose shingle. Walking on the beach was always difficult, and in the dark, the line of searchers looked like a group of drunks making their unsteady way forward.

To their left was the POW camp, but George could see very little of it. Occasionally a torch beam would swing higher and, just for a second, would illuminate one of the huts. There was no sign of life.

'I was surprised to see that that there are some Jerrys still in the camp. I thought they'd all gone?' George said.

'Just three left,' the Sergeant said. 'They want to stay here.'

'What in the village? Surely not,' George said.

'Maybe, or somewhere else in England. They are not all bad you know. It's just like us. Some bad, some good. In my line of work, I get to see plenty of bad.'

The Sergeant's words made George feel uneasy. For a second he saw himself as a grumpy, bigoted old man. Something he never wanted to be. That's what the war does to you, he thought and changed the subject.

'It was further along the beach,' he said.

'The tide is coming in, and you said it was still in the shallow surf,' said the Sergeant. 'A body could easily be moved along the beach in these conditions. We will need to be patient.'

George thought of hot stew and mashed potatoes.

The search seemed to go on forever, but eventually, it was found, bobbing around in the slightly deeper water. Two policemen in Wellington boots walked into the restless water and pulled the body ashore. George looked the other way.

A young Constable and George walked back to the car, with hardly a word exchanged between them. George was driven home to Mary and his much-needed stew.

The police Sergeant called the next day to thank George for reporting and assisting them in recovering the body. He said that they would be in touch if they needed any further information from George and Mary. He left his name, Sergeant Fred Johnson, and a telephone number if they needed to speak to him about the case. His tone suggested that he would rather they didn't call and, as far as George was concerned, he would be happy not to hear anything ever again about the case.

But strangely, as time passed, George and Mary found that they did want to know who the body on the beach was. After six months had passed, George decided to give Sergeant Johnson a call, just to satisfy his curiosity. He was told that Johnson had retired. He had apparently reached retirement age in 1941, but had agreed to stay on because of the lack of experience in the local force.

George said that nobody else could help and rang off. He then tried to put it out of his mind, and it was about two years before they walked Gracie on the beach. Then one sunny July day they decided to try again. The POW camp had almost been demolished and a few holidaymakers in caravans and tents had taken its place. It brought that awful night back again, but he didn't mention it to Mary.

Then another year went by, and George was sitting in the local pub. It was Thursday and Darts night. George didn't play anymore, because of a touch of arthritis, but he liked to watch his pub team play. Tonight, it was a team from a pub in nearby King's Lynn. It was a close match, with the visitors winning by a small margin.

As was customary, the losers bought a round for the winning team, and there was a good deal of banter. A man from the visiting team walked away from the noisy crowd and sat down next to George.

'It's George, isn't it. George Kisby,' he said.

He was a tall, well-built man and his voice was familiar. 'You might not remember me, but I remember you. It was my job to remember faces, and I remember you, George. He held his hand out and said, 'Sergeant Fred Johnson. That was a terrible night for you at the beach.'

It suddenly clicked in George's memory. The voice was familiar, but it had been so dark that he had not been able to see the Sergeant's face properly, just glimpses from the headlights and torches.

'Sorry, I didn't recognise you. Just your voice. I thought I had heard it somewhere before,' said George, almost flinching at the big man's handshake.

Johnson pointed to the other end of the bar, which was empty. 'Let's go and talk over there where it's quieter.' They took their pints and moved away.

As soon as they sat down, Johnson began to explain what had happened.

'I wanted to let you know that we hadn't even been able to identify the poor bugger,' he said. 'Not a clue, not a bit of identity on him. Even the clothing labels had been cut out. He had been stabbed several times with a seven-inch blade, but that was of no use to us.'

'Didn't anyone report him missing?' asked George.

'No, not a single enquiry that matched his description. But that is not so surprising in these times when whole families have been wiped out in the bombings. I think he must have been from somewhere way beyond our patch. London, Birmingham, Coventry, who knows?' Johnson sat back and took a long gulp of beer.

'The wife and I often speculated just who he was. Somebody's brother or son. Someone's boyfriend. Such a dreadful thing…' George said quietly, almost to himself.

'Yes, he was only a young chap. Twenty-five, twenty-six.' agreed the Sergeant. 'Whoever did it, was determined that they were not going to get caught. Very careful and very clever. They had even cut the ends of his fingers off.'

Johnson stopped himself immediately he saw the horror on George's face.

'We're pretty sure it was done after he was murdered.' Johnson added quickly. This time it was George who needed a good drink from his glass.

'It's hard to believe this could happen here,' George said and then took another swig of his beer.

'Don't worry George,' Johnson said. 'It almost certainly didn't happen anywhere near here. We think he was killed and then brought here, taken out in a boat, and thrown overboard. He hadn't been in the water for very long. People who know the Wash well think that the plan was to let the outgoing tide take the body to the North Sea. They may have got there late or early for some reason, or simply didn't understand the tide and currents of the Wash. Whatever they thought, they got it wrong. The Wash is a difficult water to predict, even when you know it well.'

'Do you think they will ever be caught?' asked George, wishing he had a happier story to tell Mary when he got home.'

Sergeant Johnson gave a pained smile. 'Maybe, maybe not. There's nothing much the lads can do, except hope for a lucky break. The case has been put away now, but it could be opened again.' He drained his beer glass and stood up. 'Anyway, I am retired now, and there is nothing I can do about it. I'm glad I've had the chance to tell you what has happened. And don't worry. As they say, lightning never strikes twice in the same place.

CHAPTER 2

September 1961

Emily Miller sat at her small desk looking through back copies of the local newspaper. Her desk, which was actually a table, was jammed up against the glass and wood partition which formed one side of the newsroom. In effect, she was sitting in the corridor. People hurried past her all day long, some called a cheery hello to her as they swept passed, but most just swept by. She felt like a schoolgirl who had been banished from the classroom for disruptive behaviour.

But Emily was happy. She had only decided that she wanted to be a journalist after she left school, but as soon as she began to find out more about it, no other work was going to be good enough for her. And this was the first step on the ladder. It was a year ago that she got the trainee journalist job, thanks to her good friend and mentor Geoff Upthorne. A former editor of the newspaper and then a lecturer in journalism, Emily met Upthorne at the college in Hertfordshire where she was studying. He told her about the job in Peterborough and then recommended her to the current editor.

She dearly wanted to take her place amongst the other journalists, just the other side of the partition, but at the moment there wasn't enough space. What space would she take up? She was more of an obstacle in the corridor than she would be in the office.

Emily was a slim girl and only just over 5ft tall. She had a very expressive face that often gave away her feelings. Her pert nose and full lips gave her a look of vulnerability, but her searching dark brown eyes could be unnerving for anyone who was not being honest with her. One moment she could be looking serious and earnest, but in a split second she could light up a room with her big smile.

She was aware that being female was an obstacle she had yet to get over, but being small seemed to make building trust with the other journalists even more difficult. Most of them were very nice to her, but they made her feel a little like a new pet the office had acquired.

She was also very attractive, with dark brown hair, which she wore in a fashionable ponytail. She often thought that many of her male colleagues seemed to think that if you were in any way pretty, you could certainly not be intelligent as well. Once again, she was okay with this. When she eventually got the chance, she would show them just what a good journalist she could be.

'Em,' a voice bellowed from inside the newsroom.

She looked up to see John Cadham waving a piece of paper in her direction. He had not even bothered to look up to see if she had heard him. John

Cadham was her immediate boss. He was a senior and very experienced journalist, who at some time during the twenty years he had been in the business, had lost all interest in the job.

His life was now dedicated to doing as little as possible and passing anything that looked like a problem to anyone he could find. By about 11 o'clock he would be heading for the Bull Hotel Bar, supposedly to meet people who could put him on to a good story. But the good stories never seemed to appear.

She hated him calling her Em. Only family and close friends could do that, so she waited.

'Emily, will you get your arse in here?' He shouted again. She smiled to herself as she stood up and walked through to where he was sitting.

'Has anyone told you that you are an ignorant pig?' she said as she arrived at his desk. She had learnt very quickly that there was nothing John enjoyed more than exchanging insults. Emily thought that he had never shaken off his teenage mentality, even though he was now over forty.

'Yes, almost everyone I know has,' he giggled with pleasure. 'So, Emily.' He emphasised her name, 'could you be kind enough to look after this for me, and stop pissing about.' He waved the paper again. 'I've got to go out,' he added.

'Yes, the Bull should be open by now,' she said with a smile.

He handed Emily the sheet of paper with a grin. 'Go and get on with some work, you cheeky little bugger.' He picked up his jacket and walked out ignoring the banter from all sides of the office.

The letter was addressed to the editor and was written in a spidery scrawl that waved up and down on each line. It was written on cheap thin paper, of the size that came with a purpose made letter pad, but the handy sheet of lined paper had obviously not been used.

As far as Emily could make out from the scrawl, it was written by a woman called Janet Burrows. She had gone to live in Northern Ireland just after the end of the war. There was a boyfriend she had before the war that she had lost touch with. He had been called up in 1939, and now she was back in Peterborough, she was hoping to meet up with him again. The few people that knew him said he never returned. They think that he must have gone somewhere else, or maybe met someone else while he was abroad. Janet says that if he had returned, she was sure he would have tried to contact her. Could the paper help her to find him? His name was Harry Smithson.

Emily walked down to a room that was generally referred to as Pete's Parlour. It was the in-house library and archive. It was stuffed full of reference books, national newspapers, trade and technical magazines, plus many other reference sources. Pete was a quietly spoken old guy, who had been running the library for many years and looked older than most of the books. He was tall, thin and walked with a stoop. Steel rimmed glasses were permanently perched on the end of his nose, and occasionally, he would put on an additional pair to read very small print. His long grey cardigan hung limply on his scrawny shoulders, and he always shuffled around in slippers.

Pete looked a mess, but he could usually find, within seconds, what you wanted.

He was sitting at the huge table that almost filled the library. He looked up and peered over both pairs of glasses. 'Hello Emily, what are you looking for?'

'I've got this letter,' she said, placing it on the table.' A woman has asked us if we can help find her missing boyfriend. It seems that he didn't return from the war.'

'And she only just noticed. That was sixteen years ago?' Pete said with a grin.

'She said she went to live in Northern Ireland and has only just come back,' Emily explained. 'I know it sounds odd and I will go and see her to find out more, but in the meantime, I thought I'd better check if he is listed as being demobbed.'

'Okay,' said Pete, 'I should start with a call to the Ministry of Labour, it used to be the Ministry of Labour and National Service until 1959. They ran the whole demobilisation process and will have the records. There is a London telephone directory over there.' He pointed to a shelf on the other side of the room.

'Thanks, Pete, I knew you would have the answer,' she said, giving him one of her best smiles.

'Don't take the directory away,' he said.

Several telephone calls to various government departments later and she had the answer. Harry Smithson had been demobbed on the 15th September 1946. His address was just shown as Peterborough, which Emily was told was not uncommon for those being demobbed. Many didn't know if they had a home to go to or if they were going to be welcomed.

The next thing, Emily thought, was to go and have a chat with Janet. The address on the letter was in Cromwell Road, which Emily knew was within walking distance from the office. She reached the street and quickly realised that Janet's home was at the other end of the road. It was the middle of the day, and the street was quiet. The people were mainly elderly locals, but there were also several Asian and West Indian children playing in the road. She found the house number and knocked on the door, which was in the centre of a small Victorian terrace. A young woman opened the door. She was holding a baby in her arms.

'Janet?' Emily asked.

'No, she's upstairs. I'll knock.' She turned and knocked on a second door that had been fitted at the bottom of the stairs, making the house into two flats.

'It's for you Janet,' she shouted.

'Okay,' came the reply.

The woman turned to leave, but the baby was making noises, smiling and holding her arms out towards Emily.

'She seems very happy,' Emily said.

'She is as long as I am carrying her about,' said the woman as she shut the door to her flat.

Janet could have been fifty, but Emily felt sure she was a lot younger than that. Her face, and particularly her eyes, looked tired and worn down by life. But her body and movement suggested a younger person. Her clothes were old and drab, and she had a nasty looking scar on her forehead.

'I'm Emily Miller, from the newspaper. You wrote to us about Harry Smithson.'

'Have you found him?' she asked.

'No, I just need to talk to you and get all the details before I write the story and put the appeal in the paper,' explained Emily.

She seemed surprised. 'Oh, I thought you would just put it in. I didn't expect… well, you to call,' she said.

'We have to check. You never know why people might want to find someone. It could cause a lot of problems. People could even be put in danger.'

Emily hadn't expected the woman to be so nervous about her coming to meet her.

'Yes, I suppose so. You'd better come in.'

Janet led the way upstairs and into a sparsely furnished living room. Janet sat on a battered wood chair that had been painted pale blue, but most of the colour had worn off. Emily sat opposite on a round seated kitchen stool. The table was a card table with a small table cloth on it.

'I am sorry for this,' Janet said, waving a hand at the room. 'I'm trying to get some stuff together.'

'It's no problem at all. I'm sorry if I've upset you, dropping in on you like this,' Emily said. 'When I read your letter, I wanted to help you as much as I could. I thought you would be pleased.'

'I am pleased,' said Janet. 'you just took me by surprise. I am very grateful that you are trying to help me.' Janet spoke in almost a whisper, her eyes focused on the small table between them.

'Tell me about Harry,' Emily said.

'Before the war, we were very close. We were both very young. I was sixteen and Harry was nineteen. My parents were pleased to see the back of me. We were a big family, seven kids. I was the eldest and fed up with looking after the others. I think I was a real little sod.'

'Where are your parents now?' Emily asked.

'They moved away. I don't know where. We lost touch. And I wouldn't want to see them again. I don't want them to know that I've made a total mess of my life.' She sighed and put her head in her hands.

'Did you and Harry move in together?' Emily asked.

'Yes, in here. Julie's parents bought the house and turned it into two flats. She was just a little kid then. Harry and me rented this one. Harry could turn his hand to most things, so although he never had a steady job, we were not often short of money.

'He came from Wisbech and knew a lot of people there. So there was always plenty of land work and general labouring for him. Then the war came along, and he was called up. Harry wasn't good at writing, or reading for that matter. He was clever, but not with that sort of thing. He was big and strong, and a hard worker, but writing letters was a problem.

'He tried, but gradually the letters got less, and then I didn't hear from him at all. I kept hoping for a year or two, but nothing came. So when I got the opportunity to go and live in Northern Ireland, with some relatives, I thought I would go. Then the war came to an end, and I thought I might hear from him. But I didn't,' her voice trailed off, and Emily realised that she was crying.

Emily was not good with people crying. It wasn't encouraged in her family. You were told to pull yourself together and get over it, but she thought to say that would be a little harsh under the circumstances.

'Well,' said Emily, 'let's try and look on the bright side. There is a good chance that Harry is somewhere around and he will hear about the story in the paper. He's probably embarrassed that he didn't keep up the correspondence with you and thought you didn't want to see him.'

Janet looked up at Emily. 'So you think there is a chance that he will come forward?'

'Every chance', said Emily. 'The power of the press and all that. I am sure somebody will know where he is.'

CHAPTER 3

Emily wrote a small piece about Harry Smithson and asked for anyone who knows where he might be, to get in touch with the newspaper. She waited expectantly for a telephone call or a letter, but none came. She was beginning to forget about it altogether when the receptionist at the office called Emily to say there was a lady in reception asking to speak to her.

She went down to meet her and was surprised to see that it was Julie from the downstairs flat, complete with baby in a pram. She took her into the small room next to the reception desk, which was reserved for impromptu meetings.

'Hello Julie, I didn't expect it to be you,' Emily said. 'Janet told me about you and the flats belonging to your parents.'

'Yes, she said she did,' said Julie. 'But from reading the story in the paper, I wondered if she had mentioned Billy Pope. Because if anything did happen to Harry, I think he would be the first on my list of likely suspects?'

'Who's Billy Pope?' Emily asked.

'Billy Pope is a nasty piece of work and a real knob,' Julie said with venom. 'She moved in with Harry to start with. I was just five at the time, so I didn't take much notice. But my parents used to say he was Okay. A big chap. Looked like a giant to me,

29

but I was only small. Then the war came, and he was called up. A few months later and Billy Pope arrived on the scene.'

The baby started to make whining noises, and Julie stood up, lifted her out of the pram, and sat down with the baby on her lap. She bounced it gently a few times on her knee, and the grizzling stopped.

Emily thought she ought to say something nice about the baby, but she had never been very good at small talk, particularly about babies. She often thought about a time in the future, when she might want babies of her own. Trouble was she could not comprehend, wanting a baby. They seemed to be a lot of trouble to her. But she supposed it must be one of those things you grow into.

'She's very good,' was all she could come up with.

'Yes, but I can't let her start crying. Once started she can go on for hours,' Julie said.

'What's her name?' Emily was relieved to think of that one.

'Jennifer,' said Julie, looking proudly at her offspring.

Okay, that's enough of that thought Emily. 'You were telling me about Billy.'

'Yes, he was constantly in trouble. The police were at the door all the time; asking about stolen goods, fights, nicked cars. He was a little, wiry, rough looking type. Really cocky. And he used to knock Janet about. My Dad was always saying he was going to do something about Billy. Get them thrown out. But I think they were sorry for Janet and scared of what Billy might do. He always carried a knife and, from what we heard, wasn't slow in using it.'

Jennifer began to grizzle again. Julie bounced her gentle up and down on her knee. Jennifer giggled and waved her arms around in delight.

'Then one day, near the end of the war they were gone. I was ten and beginning to understand the problems that Billy Pope had caused my parents. My Dad began to smile again. I know many people must have felt that way because the war was coming to an end, but I think most of his mood change was because Billy Pope had gone.'

All the time Julie had been talking, Emily was taking shorthand notes. She had taught herself to just glance down quickly at her notes. She wanted to look people in the eye when they were talking. That way she felt she could judge if they were telling the story as it was or how they would have liked it to be. What Julie was saying reflected the true misery that one bad person can bring to several people's lives.

'When did you hear from them again?' she asked.

'Not till last month, when Janet wrote to my Dad asking if she could come back. She said that she had broken it off with Billy. Dad always had a soft spot for her. He knew she had a rough time with Billy and always said that it couldn't last. One day she would realise what she was doing with her life. As it happened, the flat was empty. He and my mum had moved out and left me in the downstairs flat. Dad's job had changed, and he went to work at a factory near Newcastle. He asked me if I didn't mind Janet coming back and I said it was okay by me, as long as Billy Pope stayed away.'

'She had told him that Billy had gone off with another woman about a year ago. I didn't know her that well to trust what she said, but I know my Dad well enough, and he's a good judge of people. I also knew he was worried about me being on my own in the house, with just Jennifer for company.'

'How did you finish up on your own with Jennifer?' Emily asked.

'Through not listening to my Dad,' she replied. 'I was twenty-two when he went to work up north. He wanted me to go with them and said he would then rent out both flats.'

'And at twenty-two, you thought here's a chance to get some real independence,' Emily said. 'I would have felt just the same.'

'Yes, I had a good job at a hairdressers in town, and I had just found a new boyfriend, who I was crazy about. I dug my heels in and said I was going nowhere. So, they moved north, and Bernard moved in with me. We had two wonderful years, I got pregnant, and Bernard told me he still loved me, but he couldn't deal with a baby. And he was gone,' she said bitterly. 'Dad always said there was something not right with him.'

Julie bounced the baby again and said, 'I'm not trying to cause any trouble for Janet. Since she came back, she has been a real friend to me, but I can't understand why she didn't tell you about Billy. It was one of the main things that my Dad worried about during the war. What happens when Harry comes back, and Billy is still hanging around?

'There was bound to be trouble, and I know Janet worried about it. Did Billy do anything to Harry without Janet knowing? Does she know something? Has Billy gone for good or does he have some sort of hold on her,' Julie looked as though she was about to cry.

'Julie, I know how difficult this must have been for you to tell me about this. But it was essential that you did. I will talk to the people here with more experience than me, and we will work out a way to get to the truth.'

Emily saw Julie and Jennifer to the door and assured them that everyone would be okay. She wished that she could feel as confident as she sounded. The only colleague she should discuss this with is John Cadham, and that would be as useful as talking to the office cat. Eventually, she would have to go to the police, but at the moment everyone was just guessing at what might have happened. Billy Pope was probably living happily in Ireland, with a couple

of children and a lovely wife. That, she thought is
wishful thinking.

CHAPTER 4

Emily left the story alone for a couple of days, just to see if any other ways of approaching Janet about Billy Pope came to mind. She woke up that morning knowing that the straightforward way was the best. Just a little white lie to make Julie's surprise visit seem innocent, as indeed it was. It might just have seemed to be a little underhand from Janet's point of view, but if she genuinely had nothing to hide, it wouldn't be a problem.

She was, however, a little apprehensive as she knocked quietly on Julie's door. She must have been watching through the window because it opened immediately.

'Hello Julie. I want to speak to Janet,' she said quietly, 'but I promise it will be alright.'

She nodded. 'Yes, I know you will be tactful.' Emily smiled, thinking of the many times she had been told, when it came to tact, you are like a drunk in a china shop – you don't mean any harm, but you just can't stop breaking things. And she had to admit that as soon as a question popped into her head, she often found herself asking it, without thinking about the consequences.

Julie tapped on the door and called. 'Janet, Emily from the paper is here to see you.' She then opened the door to her flat and scuttled inside.

Janet opened the door for Emily. She looked tired and red-eyed. 'Come on up,' she said and wearily climbed the stairs ahead of Emily.

'Do you have any news?' she asked, sitting down at the small table.

'I'm afraid not, but I do have one or two questions for you, and I hope they won't upset you.'

She looked at Emily for several seconds and then said. 'Someone has told you about Billy, haven't they?'

'Yes,' said Emily. 'It was quite by chance. I was going back to the office a couple of days ago, and I ran into Julie, walking Jennifer in the pushchair. I asked her if you were okay and she was telling me how nice it was to have the flat occupied by someone that she could call a friend. I think she was lonely and a bit down before you returned.

'Then she said that you had a difficult time with Billy Pope and how worried her Dad had been about you.'

Janet nodded her head, slowly and thoughtfully. 'Yes, Billy was a bastard, and I should have dumped him then, while I was living here. He could be okay, in his wild sort of way. And I guess that I loved to be out with him. It's pathetic now, but I actually liked the way that everyone was wary of him. Even the hardest men gave him respect. It sounds so stupid now, but when I was young, I didn't even think about how wrong it was. And at the same time as loving this attention, I was scared to death. I couldn't see a way of dumping him, not without a massive bust up.'

'Why did you decide to go to Ireland?' asked Emily.

'He had relatives there, and I was scared that when Harry came back, there would be real trouble. Harry was not aggressive, but was a big man, a good boxer and not used to backing down. Billy was just a complete nutter, that was the trouble. He never knew when to stop. Never had any feelings for anyone.

'I thought the best way was to get well away from here. He wouldn't even consider it at first, but then one day the police were getting very close about something dodgy he had been doing, and suddenly Billy was keen to get to Ireland.'

'How did you manage to get rid of him in Ireland?' Emily asked, sitting down in the chair opposite.

'In the end, it was easy. He found someone else, and I was the one to be dumped. He just threw me out with all my belongings in a carrier bag. Fortunately, Billy was never mean with money. He always had plenty and always gave me more than enough. Money was always his way of saying sorry after he had given me a beating.

'I just knew that he would get fed up with me eventually, in fact, I didn't think it would be so long. He just came home one day and said that he had found someone else. I almost laughed with relief, but I said nothing and got out as quickly as I could. I had decided some years before to build myself a little nest egg. It gave me enough money to get a room in Ireland. I lived there until I found somewhere back here. It took some time because at first, I didn't know who to turn to. Then I thought of Julie's Dad and how good he was to me before. I contacted him, and he said yes.'

'Why didn't you tell me this when we first met?' asked Emily.

'It's very difficult for me to explain, but I think that Billy may have killed Harry. He came back to England a couple of years after the war had ended. He said he had to clear up some business. I thought it was strange and then it occurred to me. Had he come back here to take Harry out of the scene, so that we could come back. He didn't seem to like it in Ireland. I think that the hard men out there were in a different league to him. And that hurt his ego. The decent people there didn't like him either, and I think they only tolerated him because his relatives were well-liked.

'I also thought that I would be dragged into things if he had come back and killed Harry. People were bound to think that I had planned all this with Billy. After all, it didn't take me long to let him move in after Harry was called up. And I still don't know why I did. I was young and stupid and, to be honest, I thought that Harry would get killed in the war. He was stupidly brave. He was just the sort to be leading the charge. He seemed to have no fear. But he was so much kinder than Billy could ever be.

'Now I want to know if Billy did come back and kill him. I want to know, and I will gladly come forward and tell everything I know about Billy Pope.'

Emily sat and waited to see if there was anything else Janet had to say. She had quickly learned that listening to important answers was more important than asking lots of meaningless questions.

'I know this has been difficult for you,' Emily said at last. 'It's hard to admit the mistakes that we have made in life. I am going to do everything I can to find out what happened to Harry Smithson.'

It's all very well making these promises, Emily thought to herself, but what do I do next?

CHAPTER 5

Emily was feeling a little out of her depth. In her first year of journalism, she had dealt with lost cats and dogs, gnomes disappearing from gardens and even an escaped snake, but the scrawled letter she had been handed by John Cadham was leading her into new territory.

Her desire to get the scoop, that could suddenly make her name, was extremely strong. A dream come true at her age. That excited her. But going after people who might be capable of killing in cold blood sent alarm bells ringing inside her head. However, backing down was out of the question for Emily. She was not going to give up on her quest for success and recognition. She needed some advice from Geoff Upthorne.

Emily had made a point of keeping in touch with Geoff and his wife, Maureen. She had called them earlier to make sure they were at home. Emily had put on her new pale blue and white striped trouser suit, that she had bought on her last trip to London. It was perfect for meeting Geoff and Maureen, and she thought it made her look a little bit older. Setting out to walk to their house, which overlooked the town park, Emily felt her concerns about the story were already beginning to recede and that she had been silly to worry so much.

It was an elegant red brick home, with a large garden and huge trees that hid most of it from the road. It was a beautiful late summers day that occasionally comes along in September, and Emily had taken a short-cut through the park. It felt as if she was deep in the countryside. Birds were singing, and the last of the butterflies flitted quickly from one bush to another as if frantically working to get their tasks finished before Autumn set in.

Geoff and Maureen were waiting for her on the patio of their beautiful garden. They sat in old wicker chairs around a low table, with what looked like cold lemonade in a large jug. Geoff, with his old battered Panama hat and Maureen in a little floppy white cotton hat, perched on top of her head.

As always, they seemed so happy and pleased to see her. Emily felt totally relaxed and free to talk about anything. Unlike her parents, she knew that they would not be judgmental and they would be perfectly honest with her if they thought she was making a mistake.

Maureen greeted Emily with a hug and a kiss and said that she was looking as lovely as ever. They asked how she was getting on with her flatmate Viv. How were her parents? And how was work going? She said Viv was great and there was never a dull moment when she was around. Her parents were fine she said, although she had not been in touch with them for a few weeks. Maureen gently scolded her about that, saying that she should go and visit them more often. She promised she would. She explained that it was work issues that she needed to discuss.

'I would welcome some advice about a story I'm working on,' she said.

Maureen smiled and stood up. 'This is when I go and get some tea ready for us. Newspaper talk, or more usually, newspaper politics, is something that I am not qualified to talk about - thankfully.' She bustled off indoors.

Geoff looked delighted to be asked, and Emily ran through the whole story so far.

'My problem is,' said Emily, 'that everything that might or might not have happened was at least fourteen years ago. People forget things in that time, and what they can't remember, they make up. And there is no proper evidence of any sort. Not even a body.'

'What does Cadham say about all this? Presumably, he gave you the letter to deal with in the first place?' Geoff asked.

'To be honest, I have not spoken to him about it. I needed to get some advice on the best way to move forward. Right now, if I asked him for help, he would just find a hundred and one reasons for leaving it alone. If I press on with it and think that there could be a really good story, he will say it's a waste of time. I know him only too well. He will leave me alone until there is some glory to be had and then he will grab it like a frog spotting a nice juicy insect.'

'Yes, I see your problem,' Geoff said. 'You do need more evidence. The body is the key. You need to check back through the archives to see if anything was reported back in 1945 or 1946.' He hesitated for a few moments and then said, 'You know, I can vaguely remember something about a body washing up on a beach somewhere near King's Lynn. I think the police were having problems identifying it. If you can find something about that you may have found your man, Harry Smith, or whatever his name was?'

'Harry Smithson,' said Emily. She felt a weight had been lifted from her. Geoff's advice and excellent memory had helped her out again. 'Thanks, Geoff, as always you have come up with a solution. I wish I could think as clearly as that.'

He laughed. 'You will. Just learn something from each job and by the time you are as old as I am you will be able to dish out advice as if you have just thought of it.'

'I don't think so,' Emily laughed.

'One more bit of advice,' said Geoff. 'Be careful about where you arrange to meet people. Always try to meet in public places and if you have any doubts about the person you are going to interview, take someone with you, even if it has to be that lazy bugger, Cadham.'

'I will. I promise,' Emily said.

'And when you have some evidence, you take it to the police. You are the one who knows all the details, and that will carry more weight. Then there can be no doubt about whose story it is.'

Emily enjoyed afternoon tea and the pleasant conversation with Geoff and Maureen. She then walked back to the office, happy to know what she had to do. As she walked, she thought about her first meeting with Geoff.

He had given a lecture at the college in Hertfordshire where she was studying. Geoff was a blunt, straight-talking Yorkshireman, who had spent all his working life in local newspapers, from tea boy to Editor. Emily had been inspired by his passionate belief in the role of local newspapers, to inform, protect and bring communities together. After the lecture, Emily had managed to talk to Geoff, and from that moment her whole attitude to her future career changed.

She had been hesitant about what she really wanted to do. Her father wanted her to study law. He was a solicitor, and he thought that she would eventually take over the family business. He had it all mapped out for her.

To Emily, it all seemed very dull. But she had no idea what else she wanted to do, so in a last-minute panic, she signed up for the journalism course. She was good at writing essays, so that must be a help, she thought.

That afternoon Emily sat and listened to Geoff give his insight on what good journalism was all about.

After he had finished the lecture, she hung around hoping for a chance to talk to him. He readily agreed and looked pleasantly surprised that she was so keen to know more. They had talked for a couple of hours before the janitor told them he had to lock up. It was mainly Geoff talking about some of the difficult assignments he had experienced during his career and quite a few hilarious ones. Geoff seemed equally impressed with the enthusiasm that Emily showed for journalism, which she failed to tell him had only happened after hearing his lecture that afternoon. It was some months later she told him that, until their conversation, journalism was just an escape from being a solicitor.

She arrived back at the office and found that there were only one or two people still there and, as she expected, John Cadham was not one of them. It was nearly six-o-clock. Time seemed to have flown. She walked down the corridor to Pete's Parlour. He was there, carefully sifting through a pile of papers.

Do you have copies of the King's Lynn paper, going back to 1945 and 46?

'For you and only for you Emily my dear, I will personally find them and have them laying on that table in the morning,' he said.

'Pete, you are a real star. I don't know how you do it. Do you ever go home?'

'Yes, occasionally,' he laughed.

CHAPTER 6

Pete was as good as his word and there, stacked on the large table, were piles of yellowing old newspapers. Emily had already checked that World War Two had ended in September 1945. However, a plan had been put into place in September 1944 by the Minister of Labour and National Service, Ernest Bevin, to process the demobilisation as quickly and smoothly as possible. In reality, it had been anything but quick or smooth. Returning over four million men and women to 'civvy street' was always going to be very difficult.

The process was started in June 1945 before the end of the war. Emily also knew that those who had the longest service were demobbed first, taking their age into account. As Harry Smithson had served almost all through the war, she thought she'd better start checking the newspapers from June 1945.

She thought that the story about the body found at Snettisham would be on the front page, but still decided that she ought to check all the main news pages. Although paper rationing kept sizes down during the war, there were still plenty of pages to look through. Emily stuck at the job, even though her back and neck were aching from turning the broadsheet pages over. She stood up and found that to be quicker and less wearing. She was being driven by excitement. The thought that she was going to find something that would throw some more light on the story was pushing her on. She didn't even stop for coffee.

Three hours later and after checking fourteen months of local newspapers, she, at last, found what she was looking for and what Geoff Upthorne had remembered.

It wasn't the main story, but it had prominence on the front page. It was headed 'Mystery Body Found on Snettisham Beach'. Police appeal for people to come forward and identify the body. There was also an artist's sketch, which Emily supposed was made from the corpse. It looked as though the artist did not fancy the job. It was so sketchy, it could have been anyone Emily thought.

'I've found it, Pete,' she said. He got up and walked over to where she was standing.

'Looks like a fun story you're working on Em. I take it you want a copy?'

'Yes, as quick as you can Pete.' Then she thought that sound a bit bossy, so she added. 'Yes please, that would be a great help.'

He laughed. 'You're okay Em. You're keen and you say it how it is. And that's alright by me.'

He picked the paper up and took it over to where the copying camera was standing. He turned the large lights on, which were mounted either side of the camera and took three shots of the story.

'There you go Em. I'll get it processed, and you can have a print at...' he paused to look at his watch, '...three-o-clock.'

She thanked him and made her way back to her desk.

CHAPTER 7

True to his word, Pete arrived at Emily's office in the corridor with a brown foolscap envelope in his hand. She thanked him and then pulled the photographic print out and laid it on her desk. It was a good copy of the article and sketch. Pete had trimmed it down, so that was all there was to be seen. No distractions from the surrounding content, only what Emily wanted to show Janet.

She saw John Cadham walk through the office and looking at her through the glass partition. Emily quickly put the print back into the envelope. John was now waddling down the corridor.

'What have you got there,' he called out as he made his sedate way towards her.

'Nothing to do with you,' Emily replied, putting the envelope into her bag.

'Have you made some progress with the letter about the missing boyfriend?' he asked.

He can smell a story, Emily thought. He had a sixth sense when any of the junior journalists were getting somewhere. Before you know it, all your work and effort would be on his desk. A quick subbing job on it and the story would be his. Well, not this time.

'I have made a bit of headway, but not much,' she said.

'Come on,' said Cadham. 'You have been ferreting away, in and out of the office. What have you been doing.'

'Working,' she replied, 'you should try it sometime.'

'Why should I do that when I've got an eager little beaver to do it for me,' he laughed.

'I'll let you know when I have something worth showing you,' she called over her shoulder as she walked towards the door. 'I wouldn't want to waste your time. I know you're a busy man.' Her voice, full of sarcasm.

'You're in the corridor now,' he shouted after her. 'Next stop is in the street.' But Emily had already gone.

She walked the short distance to Janet's flats and knocked. But nobody answered. She tried again. This time a little harder. A voice called 'I'm coming,' and Emily was surprised to see Janet had answered the door.

'Julie has gone shopping, and I can't hear anyone at the door when I am upstairs. We ought to get a bell.' Emily was pleased to see that Janet was looking a lot better than the broken woman she was when they first met. Maybe because things were happening at last, and because she might be getting closer to finding out what happened to Harry, Janet seemed to be getting herself together.

Emily didn't want to destroy any small hope that she might have had, but she had to ask her to look at the sketch she carried in her handbag. 'I have something to show you, but I don't want to upset you again.'

Janet turned deathly white, and the look of shock on her face showed that she had been expecting the worst and now she knew her fears were well founded. 'Come in,' she said, 'let's go upstairs.'

She sat at the small table and covered her face with her hands. 'Is it what I feared?'

'It might be. I have a sketch for you to look at. Take your time and look at it carefully.' Emily pulled the print from the envelope and laid it on the table in front of Janet. Janet stared at the artist's sketch, she said nothing, but tears were rolling down her cheeks. She shook her head as if trying to deny the truth and then made a visible attempt to pull herself together.

'Yes, that looks like Harry. I'm as certain as I can be from a drawing, that is him. I don't have any photos, because Billy burnt them all when he found them in my drawer. It is ridiculous that I am feeling so shocked and sad now. I was the one that broke off the relationship when I let Billy Pope move in with me. But I was a different person then. The thought of living through the war on my own was terrifying. And it was only when the end of the war was in sight that I began to think about Harry coming back. I felt sure I would have been told if anything had happened to him when he was away in the army.'

'Do you think he would have wanted to come back if he found out about you and Billy?' Emily asked.

'No, he probably wouldn't, but I do think he would have tried to talk to me, and that would have been enough to send Billy into one of his rages. What's done is done. I know now that I was to blame for getting into this mess. Now I need to find out if Billy is a murderer.'

'We will have to find that out,' said Emily. You're not on your own now. We can do this together.'

Emily went back to the office, marvelling at the way she could make people have such confidence in her. This was a big step forward, and she needed to think very carefully about her next move. Geoff found the way to identify the body; I think it is time to seek some more advice from him.

She called him and told him that she had found the piece about a body on the beach incident that he had remembered. It was in the King's Lynn paper, together with a sketch of the victim. She had shown it to Harry Smithson's ex-girlfriend, and she said it was almost certainly him. She asked Geoff if he thought it was time to speak to the police and if so, who was the best person to approach.

He immediately said, 'Mike Townsend. Detective Chief Inspector Mike Townsend to be correct.'

'I'll give him a call first and explain the situation.' Geoff said. 'He is a good sensible copper and believes that the press and police can get on well together. If they are honest with each other at all times, both sides can win. I worked happily with him for many years. But don't for goodness sake get that prat Cadman involved. Mike can't stand him.'

DCI Mike Townsend called Emily the following day and arranged for them to meet for a cup of tea in a café near the town bridge, well away from both the police station and the newspaper office. He explained that not everyone on the force agreed with his policy of working with the press and he knew that many journalists felt even more strongly about this sort of cooperation.

The place he had chosen looked like a greasy spoon from outside and Emily pushed the door open hesitantly. She looked at the handful of customers inside. They were mostly dressed in overalls, and all eyes seemed to be on her. Then she spotted the man in the suit on the far side of the room. That had to be him, but he was engrossed in a story he was reading in a newspaper. As she got closer, he looked up and smiled at her.

As she reached the table, he stood and shook her hand. 'You must be Emily,' he said. 'Is it my imagination or are journalists getting younger these days. No, don't say it, it's because I'm getting older.'

'I just look a lot younger than I am,' she said. As always, Emily liked to look at her best and had put on a smart, business-like skirt and jacket.

He laughed. 'I am a little embarrassed that I asked you to meet me here. We can go somewhere else.'

'There's no problem. You would be surprised at some of the places I have been in!'

Mike Townsend was a tall, thin man, with a serious demeanour. But when he smiled he became a completely different person, suddenly warm and friendly. Emily felt immediately relaxed in his company. He had a calmness about him which reassured her that they could work together. In fact, it felt very much like talking to Geoff Upthorne. No wonder they got on well.

'I've ordered some tea and biscuits,' he said. 'Is that okay with you?'

Once the waitress had delivered the tea and biscuits to the table, Emily opened her notebook and began to run through a summary of what had happened so far in her investigations. She had a list of the main points in her notebook so that nothing important was left out. He listened intently.

When she had finished talking, Mike was silent for a short while. He seemed to be weighing up what her next move should be.

'Okay,' he said at last. 'You don't have anything to prove or disprove that Billy Pope has done anything wrong, apart from continuing to be the nasty little bastard he always has been. Write the story about the body being identified by Janet Burrows and say that the police would like to interview Billy Pope so that he can be eliminated from their enquiries. I'll take care of the paperwork back at the station, and then we are all seen to be doing things properly. Write up what you've told me today because we can use that as a statement from you if the case goes further.'

'I'll do that as soon as I get back, 'Emily said. 'We don't know if Billy is still in Ireland or if he has come back here.'

'He will soon get to know that we are looking for him,' said Townsend. 'There are so many slimy little sods who love to toady round Billy, just to get a pat on the head from him. Wherever he is, he will soon know. Now let's get stuck into these biscuits, I just can't resist Custard Creams.'

'It's Jammy Dodgers for me,' said Emily, feeling that, once again, a good way forward had been found, without any compromises.

CHAPTER 8

She walked back to the office with a spring in her step. She liked and trusted Mike Townsend. What he said made sense and working together would bring results far more quickly. In her mind, she was writing the story about the identification of Harry Smithson and sending a message out to Billy Pope that they were on to him. This could go some way to keeping him away from Janet.

It was three-o-clock, and she felt sure that she could write this up and get it in tomorrow's edition. It was a warm afternoon now, and the town was quiet. She hurried along the pavement in Bridge Street and across the marketplace, and she even broke into a gentle trot, which wasn't easy in her new stiletto shoes.

Back in the corridor office, the air was hot and stuffy. Emily sat down and typed quickly and accurately. She had already sorted out the points that she needed to bring out in the story. She read it through for typos and to see if there was any way it could be improved. This was the most important story that she had handled, and she was reluctant to let it go, without a final read through.

Timing was important. She had to let John Cadham look at it before it was passed to the sub-editors. If she went to him too soon, he would start to alter it and then claim it as his. If she left it too late, he would have gone home. At 4.15pm she took it through into the other office.

The usual late afternoon rush was in full swing. Except at the Cadham desk, where he was sitting back in his chair, with his feet on the desk, reading the sports pages of The Daily Mirror.

He must have seen Emily coming towards him because without looking up he said, 'I'm busy.'

'Yes, I can see you are. I'll take this straight through to the subs then,' she said.

'No you bloody won't,' Cadham said, dropping his feet to the floor and snatching the story from her. He quickly read the piece. He nodded his head approvingly. 'Excellent,' he said.

For a moment, Emily was elated. At last Cadham had acknowledged her work. Then he wrote across the bottom of the page, 'by John Cadham.'

'What is that?' she asked incredulously.

'Trainees don't get bylines,' he said with a laugh.

'Who says,' said a furious Emily.

'I do,' he said, levering his bulk out of the chair and striding off to the sub-editors' room.

The flat that Emily shared with Viv was on the top floor of a large Victorian house about half a mile from the office. It had a small living room, two even smaller bedrooms, a bathroom, and a tiny kitchen. But collectively it made a decent flat for the girls.

There wasn't a huge amount to keep clean, but there was enough room for a little privacy. Viv was four years older than Emily and a lot worldlier. But they got on well together as soon as they met. Viv also worked for the paper, selling display ads.

News travelled quickly that there was a new girl in the newsroom and Viv sought Emily out just three days after she had joined the paper. Emily was still living at a B&B in the town, and Viv asked her if she would like to share a flat with her. Viv and her boyfriend had lived there together, but a mighty bust up between them had seen the boyfriend storm out, and Viv was left with a flat she couldn't afford. It had been that way for a month, and she was getting desperate.

Emily was far from happy with her B&B accommodation, and Viv's invitation was warmly accepted. Viv was an easy-going extrovert, always looking for a good time. But she sometimes had an explosive temper if things didn't go her way. But Emily's much quieter temperament and thoughtfulness were an ideal match for flatmates.

Now and again Viv's ex-boyfriend would turn up, and they would have a good row. Emily would quickly retire to her bedroom when this happened. She would put an LP on her Dansette record player and wait for the storm to pass. It always did. Usually within an hour and all was quiet again.

Two nights after the story of Harry Smithson's identification, Emily was walking home later than usual and the late September day had faded into night. She had sat and fumed for two days about Cadham and what he had done with her story. He had stolen it and had actually thought what he had done was funny. Emily decided that she was not going to let it pass. She would get her own back. It may not be immediately, but she would do it.

Thinking it through, the first thing she must do was to make sure there was nothing that he could use against her. The little jobs that he passed through to her on a regular basis had mounted up a bit while her attention had been on Billy Pope. She pulled the in-tray across to the centre of her desk and worked steadily through them until they were all done or filed.

It was nearly eight-o-clock when she finished. She grabbed her bag and walked out onto the street. Walking the half mile home was a regular occurrence for Emily, but tonight she felt strangely uneasy. She kept glancing over her shoulder. Was someone following her? No, she was just being stupid. The street lighting was barely adequate on the wide road, and there were few people about. She had never felt nervous like this before though, but each time she glanced round, everything seemed to be normal.

Nevertheless, she was very relieved to get back to the flat. She opened the large oak front door, which was shared by three flats. Then she noticed the small black car, which was parked outside the front of the house. Must be visitors to one of the other flats in the house. She closed the door as quietly as she could. All was quiet inside. The ground floor and first-floor flats were large and expensive. The one that she shared with Viv was probably where the servants used to live.

The people that lived in the large flats were middle aged, had big cars parked on the drive and always seemed very suspicious of Viv and Emily. Viv put it down to them being snobs. Emily would never say so, but she thought it was more to do with the noisy rows Viv had with her boyfriend.

She climbed the stairs and opened the door to the flat. Viv shouted, 'About time too, your visitor has been here for ages.'

Visitor, thought Emily, suddenly going cold with fear. She pushed the door open and to her great relief there sat Terry, Emily's boyfriend.

'Who forgot she was going to the pictures tonight?' Viv said with great delight.

The walk home in the darkening evening and her sensing someone was following her had really got to Emily. She was so relieved that she almost forgot to apologise.

'Sorry Terry, I completely forgot,' she said. 'It has been a really bad day. Well that's not altogether true, it started okay, but this evening has gone downhill fast.'

Terry, who made no secret of the fact that he was head over heels in love with Emily, just smiled at her as she sat down next to him on the sofa. Terry was a good, kind man and Emily valued him as a friend, but she was not totally sure about the love bit. She was trying, but somehow, he never quite managed to live up to her vision of the man who was right for her.

He was three years older than her and was a newly qualified accountant. He was intelligent, good looking and she was sure that he was destined to have a successful life. But he lived in a world that was so different from hers. It was a much more ordered and precise world. Sometimes she envied that, but she knew that she was hooked on the unpredictable, often chaotic world of journalism. And her dream was to work for a big national newspaper and write stories that were about important issues.

'When you came in you looked as though you were being chased by the hounds of the Baskerville,' Viv laughed.

'Yes, it's ridiculous. I didn't even see anyone. I just had a feeling that someone was following me.'

'And what about the rest of the day. What happened to make it so bad?' Terry asked.

She told them how Janet Burrows had written to the paper asking for its help in finding what had happened to her old boyfriend. She told them about finding the story of the body on the beach at Snettisham and how it had enabled Janet to identify the victim. Also, how Janet suspected her more recent ex-boyfriend and how she was worried that he might come back to Peterborough. She also mentioned how the police had suggested she might like to write in her story that they were interested in speaking to Billy Pope, although she did not mention which police officer it was.

'Bloody hell,' said Viv, 'do you think this Billy bloke has come back? Do you think it was him following you?'

'I don't know. I didn't see anyone, but I think it's possible that he will come back.'

'You have to be careful,' Terry said to Emily. 'These louts are complete morons. There is no telling what they might do.'

'I know,' said Emily thoughtfully. 'I will be careful from now onwards.'

'But I still haven't told you what really pissed me off,' said Emily, suddenly remembering why she was so angry.

She told them about Cadham putting his name to the story that she had just written and then taking it straight through to the sub-editors.

'The crafty bugger,' said Viv. 'That's just like him. What are you going to do about it?'

'Nothing at the moment, but I will get him back. That's why I'm late. I decided to clear up the backlog of work that had built up since he put me on this missing person story. It is all cleared up now, so he can have no complaints. And next time he wants me to cover for him or get him out of the shit, it will be sorry John. Get out of it yourself.'

'Trouble is,' said Viv. 'He's world class at getting out of the shit.'

'I'll wait my time, and I will get him,' said Emily.

'I think you need to get some rest,' Terry said. He stood up and smiled down at Emily. 'Are you still alright for the dance at the Corn Exchange on Saturday night,' he said.

'Yes,' replied Emily. 'I'm looking forward to it. And sorry about tonight.'

'Just you be careful,' he said. 'Next time you get stuck at work after dark, give me a ring, and I will come and get you. I've got a car now?

'So that's your car parked in the front,' she said.

'Yes, did you like it. Now I'm fully qualified I thought I could buy a car. What did you think to it?'

'It looked great,' Emily said, 'and I'm really sorry. I'll see the car on Saturday.' Terry had obviously brought the car round for her to see and she had spoilt the surprise.

CHAPTER 9

Emily slept fitfully that night. Bad dreams and real fears kept her awake. As always, in the hour just before dawn it was even worse. She was going to hand her notice in and see if she could still get a place studying Law. Journalism wasn't worth the hassle. And John Cadham stealing her story was the last straw. And there was letting Terry down by not being there to see his new car. She would ring her father in the morning and grovel.

But after a shower, a bowl of cornflakes and a cup of coffee she was fighting fit again. Viv helped with her tirade of what she thought of Cadham and the number of people she was going to tell what he had done. That would surely stop him doing it again. Emily knew only too well that it wouldn't have any effect at all. He was too thick skinned for that.

But Emily was still feeling better as she ran down the stairs and nearly collided with the rather austere looking woman who lived with her red-faced, grumpy husband in the ground floor flat.

'Oh, sorry,' called Emily as she went out the front door.

It was just after 8.30 in the morning and the traffic into town was beginning to build up. As Emily debated with herself whether to cross the road now or wait until she got into the city centre, she noticed a man across the road who seemed to be looking at her. At first, she thought it was someone she knew. But she couldn't place him. Then he turned away and pretended to study something in the front garden of the house opposite. He was a big man, around six feet two or three and very heavily built. He had a ruddy complexion and closely shaven grey hair.

She walked briskly along the road, now and then taking a quick look behind her. She had decided to wear her new drain-pipe jeans that she had bought in early summer but had never worn. Together with her white pumps, the outfit not only looked very fashionable, but was also very practical should she need to move quickly, particularly after her nervy walk home last night.

There was no doubt that he was following her, but he wasn't good at it. Carrying about eighteen stone around meant that his plodding steps were certainly not going to keep up with Emily. She had the advantage of being, not only half his weight, but she was also a keen hockey player. The flying winger for her school team and she had even played for the county side on a few occasions.

So, she decided to change up a gear and turn her brisk walk into a steady jog. By the time she reached the Crescent railway bridge, he was out of sight.

When she got to the office she sat down, marvelling at her tidy desk. Now she knew that she was being followed, but if they couldn't move quicker than the man that had the job today, she wasn't going to be in much danger. She could guess that this was something to do with Billy Pope. She really ought to warn Janet, but it would be silly to go to see her. It would just let them know that Janet had gone back to her old flat.

She wrote a brief note to Janet saying that she believed Billy was back in town and that it would be a good idea if she were to stay indoors for a while. Emily asked Janet to tell Julie to do the same. In the meantime, she would be speaking to the police and asking them to give Janet and Julie some protection until Billy Pope was safely behind bars. If they did need anything, they should use the local shop.

Emily then went along the corridor to Pete's Parlour. He was there, wearing carpet slippers, a long grey cardigan and the usual two pairs of glasses perched on the end of his nose. He looked up from his work and smiled at Emily.

'Hello Em, it's always good to see you. How can I help?'

'Morning Pete. I am hoping that you can find a mug shot for me.'

'I can try.'

'You know the body on the beach story that I've been working on?'

'The one that John Cadham has hijacked?'

Emily looked at him in surprise. Then suddenly said, 'Viv's been to see you?'

'How did you guess?' Pete said with a smile.

'Good old Viv,' said Emily, 'Always ready to fan the flames. Anyway, that is the story, and I would like a pic of Billy Pope. He seems to cause trouble wherever he goes, and I thought we must have at least one shot of him on file.'

'Yes, I feel sure we have. I'll dig one out and bring it along to you.'

'No, just give me a call on the internal phone and I will come and collect it.' Emily knew that Pete hated to leave his precious archives. 'I think Billy Pope is back in town and he seems to be looking for me. It's probably because I have linked his name with the Harry Smithson murder. Anyway, if he is around again I would like to see what he looks like, so I can be prepared.'

'For what?' said Pete.

'For deciding which way to run and how fast.' She laughed, but that was just bravado. The fear inside her was only just being contained.

She then walked through to the transport department and asked a driver who she knew slightly if he could drop off the note to Janet when he went out to deliver today's evening paper. He said he delivered to the corner shop near to that address and was only too pleased to help.

Emily went back and saw that Cadham had dropped a few small jobs on her desk. She looked through the glass partition to where he sat at his desk.

He had half turned his back on her and was closely studying something. Could it be that he was a little remorseful about the by-line? No, it was more likely that Viv had told him just what she thought of him.

She then called DCI Mike Townsend on the number he had given her and told him everything that had happened and her fears about Billy Pope being around again. He said he would get the beat Constables to keep an eye out for Janet and Julie and asked Emily for the address. He also told Emily to take care and when out meeting people to stick to busy public places. She assured him she would and told him that the piece about the body being identified as Harry Smithson would be out on the street at around 2 o'clock this afternoon.

She stayed at her desk for lunch, because she wasn't hungry. Then at around 1.30 pm, Pete called her to say that he had the pic of Billy Pope. She walked down to his office, and he handed her the print.

'It's a copy so that you can keep it,' said Pete.

Emily found herself staring at a thin-faced, young man, with long, lank, almost black hair. His face seemed set in a sneer. And his eyes were cold and piercing.

'Looks a nice friendly sort of chap?' Pete said.

'Police mug shots never really flatter,' said Emily, 'but he looks a real charmer.'

When Emily got back to her desk, someone had left a copy of the paper, hot off the press. She immediately looked at the front page. There was the story. 'Body Identified After 14 Years – returning soldier was stabbed and dumped into the Wash'. The subs had done a good job with the headline, and Emily thought that the whole story was one she could be proud of. But there to spoil it all was – by John Cadham.

She felt that she should go and tell him how she felt. How disappointing it was. She looked through the partition at his desk and, of course, he wasn't there. He would be in the Bull by now.

CHAPTER 10

The following morning Emily woke later than normal. She had slept well and put it down to being relieved because she had been able to share her problems with Mike Townsend and that he had responded so well. At breakfast Viv had been very funny, running through all the people she had told about Cadham's sneaky by-line. There couldn't be anyone at the paper that didn't know now.

It cheered Emily a lot that she had a friend who would stand up for her in that way. Because she was already later than her normal starting time, she walked to the office with Viv, who was almost always late. But Viv's boss never complained. Viv was by far the top ad sales person. Customers loved her larger than life personality, and she never failed to make them laugh, just before she took their order.

When Emily reached her desk, there was a note from the editor's secretary.

Betty was a tall, slim, highly efficient lady, who made the wheels turn throughout the business. She was polite but firm with everyone and very well respected. The note said simply 'John Cadham will not be in today. Come to my office and I will explain.'

Betty's office door was always open, and she waved Emily to come in as soon as she arrived. 'John Cadham will not be in for a few days,' she said, 'he is in hospital.'

'Is he ill?' asked Emily.

'He was attacked on his way home late last night by three men,' Betty said. 'They beat him up and then ran off leaving him in the street. They say that the injuries are not life-threatening, but he is badly cut and bruised, and he may have a broken rib.'

'Do they know who did it?' asked Emily

'No, I don't think so, but you know what John is like. It would be hard to find people who didn't want to punch him. I have many times,' she said without even a smile to soften the remark. 'I'm sure we will all hear about it in good time.'

Emily was wondering if she should share her suspicions about Billy Pope and the Harry Smithson murder.

Betty said, 'In the meantime, the show must go on. I'm sure you can handle things for a few days without him. And if you have any problems, anyone on the team will be very pleased to help, including me.'

With that Betty started typing at high speed, so Emily took that as the end of the conversation and went back to her desk. Several people from the news team grinned at Emily from behind the glass partition. One simply said as he walked past Emily. 'It couldn't happen to a more deserving person.'

Emily decided to stay in for lunch. She had no reason to go out, and at least she felt secure in the office.

'Em', a voice called from down the corridor. She looked up to see Pete, still in his slippers and cardigan. He waved for her to come to him. She stood up and walked towards him. He turned and walked back to the archive room.

When she reached Pete's Parlour, she could see that Pete was excited about something, so this had to be good. He didn't do excitement usually.

'Look what I have found in the files,' he said. 'I thought I remembered the name, Harry Smithson. So, I checked back through the files, especially editions round about 1937 or 38. And I found what I wanted. Unfortunately, all this does is make things more complicated.'

'In what way?' asked Emily.

'You could have another suspect in the murder of Harry Smithson.'

Pete spread the back editions across his table, carefully sorting them in date order. 'This took me until past midnight, but I think you will be interested when you see what happened.'

'Have you heard the name Arnold Lackford?'

'I've heard of Lackford the builders,' Emily replied.

'Yes, that's Arnold Lackford's business. He specialises in developing small estates of medium sized houses that appeal to up and coming young families. People who can afford to pay a bit more for segregation from the great unwashed. They offer slightly bigger, well-built houses, and add some hedges and carefully positioned trees and you have a nice private estate. This has all happened in recent times. It started in 1957 and is still just as popular in 1961. The business has boomed. He is building all over the place now.

'But it wasn't always like that. Before the war and after, he was just a jobbing builder, knocking up extensions, doing repairs, or adding a garage. That sort of thing, which was a good living no doubt, but not on the same scale as now. Nowadays, he is a big businessman, on the board of several other companies and the town council.

'In the old days, he worked alongside his men, like any small builder has to. But he was also a mouthy and opinionated thug. He drank plenty and enjoyed confrontation and a bit of a punch-up. He got banned from one or two nicer pubs, but he was a big spender, so the less selective ones would let him in.'

'Where does the link to Harry Smithson come in.' Emily asked.

Pete rubbed his hands, smiled and pulled his chair closer to the table. 'You see this first story in October 1937. In a pub in Whittlesey. The report says that a bit of banter started up between Lackford and a group of lads at the bar. The lads started to take the mickey out of Lackford, and he didn't take it well. He went over to where they were standing and tried to goad the lads to take him on in a fight. They just kept winding him up, and eventually, he took a swing at this little lad and connected with the kid's nose. He went down screaming like he had been shot.

'That was enough for Harry Smithson, who'd been standing at the edge of the crowd and was not joining in with the wind-up. He stepped over the lad, who was still screaming blue murder, and told Lackford that that was enough and that he should sit down and shut up. Lackford immediately swung a haymaker at Smithson, who calmly stepped inside it and, in quick succession threw a sharp right to the head and a left to the stomach. According to an eyewitness, that was when the fight ended, with Lackford throwing up all over the floor and unable to say anything because the wind had been knocked out of him. It turned out that Smithson was an up and coming light heavyweight boxer and quite a prospect.'

Emily was sitting at the table, listening intently to Pete's story.

'Then, a few days later the police arrested Smithson and charged him with affray and causing grievous bodily harm to Lackford,' Pete continued. 'It appears that Lackford had told the police that it was an unprovoked attack, but in the absence of any eyewitnesses coming forward, they decided to drop the charges. This wasn't surprising because the sort of people who drank in that pub were not used to telling the police anything.

'A couple of months later Lackford sued Smithson for damages. It was said that if Lackford won this case, the police would open up their case and Smithson would almost certainly go to prison. The case came to court but luckily, many of the people who were in the pub that night came forward and said that they would gladly say what happen. They put their principles behind them, stood up in court and told the truth. It hadn't been one of Lackford's regular haunts, so no one was aware of what a thug he was. Smithson was cleared of all charges and Lackford finished up with a good telling off by the judge and a big bill for court costs. Overnight Lackford had become the best joke in town.'

'He swore he would get revenge on Smithson and did manage to stop his boxing career. Lackford was close to a lot of the boxing promoters and trainers in the area. He was making good money on the side, by funding promotions and even funding some boxers. Suddenly, Smithson could not get a fight anywhere.

'He moved back to his home town of Wisbech. But Lackford had contacts there, and Smithson was attacked on numerous occasions, but generally came through with only minor cuts and bruises. But even then Lackford would not let it drop. He kept telling anyone who would listen that he would get even with Smithson one day.'

Emily looked down at the paper and said, 'You must have another source of information, in addition to the newspapers to know all that.'

'Until about an hour ago I only had what was in the papers, but then I got lucky,' said Pete, 'It was one of our delivery drivers who filled in the details for us.'

'What, one of the drivers here?' she said in surprise.

'Yes. The one you asked to deliver the note to Janet. His name's Jim. He was the kid with the broken nose. He's not forgotten what Harry Smithson did for him. Apparently, they weren't even friends, and it was the first time they had met that night.

'It's a small world.' Pete said. 'Jim just came in here to give me my copy of today's edition and saw what I was reading. He drops my copy off every day before he goes out to make his deliveries around the town, but I think this must have been the first time that something I was reading caught his eye.'

'So, good old Jim. I'll have to thank him tomorrow. I think we deserved a bit of luck, don't you?' she laughed.

'So, did the attacks eventually stop?' asked Emily.

'Jim said he lost touch with what was happening when he got a job here. There's not anymore in these back editions, but we know from your information from Janet, that Harry moved to

Peterborough and went to live with her. He could have just kept a low profile once he was here. There are more people and more places to hide.'

'Yes, and Lackford probably didn't have as many contacts here who were ready and able to take on a man like Harry Smithson,' she said. 'And then the war came, and Harry had gone.'

'Yes,' said Pete, 'and from what I hear, it was a profitable time for Lackford. He got a lot of government work, building camps and barracks, repairing damaged buildings. Then after the war there was a huge house re-building programme. He must have done well out of that. I think he came out of the war a wealthy man. That is probably when he started buying up land on which he could later build his estates.'

'I am going to sit here and write notes on all this. Then I'll go back to my desk and think what to do next,' Emily said. 'This was the last thing I expected.'

CHAPTER 11

Emily didn't take long to decide that she needed a bit of advice and in this case, she thought Mike Townsend would be the best person to help her. She called him, and they arranged to meet in Bishops Road Gardens. It was away from both the police station and the newspaper offices. It also had a wonderful view of the Cathedral, which Emily always found to be very calming. The sun shone brightly on the south side of the Cathedral, as it towered over the trees that rose above the walls of the Bishops Palace.

She was so engrossed with the view that she didn't even notice Mike Townsend until he sat down next to her. It made her jump. He shook his head and smiled.

'So Miss Miller, you took my advice about being careful,' he said.

Emily was flustered and a little embarrassed. 'I'm sorry. I have been careful, but that view of the Cathedral just distracted me.'

'Yes, it is magnificent. We take it too much for granted, so I'll forgive you being distracted,' he said.

'What did you want to talk about? Has Billy Pope been making a nuisance of himself?'

'No, I haven't seen him, but one of my colleagues at work got attacked the other night, and I think that may have been him.' Emily said.

'Yes, I heard about that,' he said. You're probably right, but he seems to have gone to ground again. All officers on duty are being told to keep a lookout, but no luck so far.'

'I wanted to talk to you about the same case. I think we might have found another suspect,' Emily said, almost apologetically.

'You are certainly prolific at finding work for the police,' he laughed.

'Yes, I am sorry, but I think that we have found someone who could be worth investigating.'

'Okay, tell me what you have found.'

Emily told him the whole story about Arnold Lackford and his feud with Harry Smithson, just as Pete had told it to her. Mike Townsend listened carefully, without interrupting her. Then he was silent for a few moments, before starting to speak.

'This is very different from the Billy Pope situation,' he said. 'Lackford may have a dodgy past, but now he is a pillar of the establishment. He has friends in high places, including the Chief Constable, who he plays golf with regularly.'

'Yes, I do understand that, but there must be something we can do.' Emily said.

'Yes, there is, but we have to go cautiously.' He took a pack of cigarettes from his pocket and offered her one.

'No thanks, I don't smoke,' she said.

He lit the cigarette, inhaled deeply and stared across the gardens.

'Suppose you report that you had asked him to comment on these allegations and give him the chance to refute them. In fact, even encourage him to deny them. Make it sound as though you're on his side.'

'Yes, I could write a piece, but in a dismissive way,' said Emily. 'Allegations have been made that a long-standing feud between murdered ex-soldier Harry Smithson and the well-respected local entrepreneur Arnold Lackford could have led to Smithson's death back in 1946. It would seem very unlikely that a man of Arnold Lackford's standing could be involved in any way. The police say that they will not comment on speculative allegations.'

He looked at Emily. 'Yes, that's just the sort of thing. There is a rumour going around, and here is your chance to put a stop to it.'

'Yes, that could work,' she said. 'And you wouldn't mind me saying that the police had refused to comment?'

'No, not at all, I always refuse to comment on such speculations,' he laughed. 'Hopefully, you will get some reaction from a story like that. Let's see what happens. Our good friend Geoff and I used that ploy on a few occasions. Sometimes it brings results, sometimes it doesn't. Lackford being a man of considerable influence and having friends in high places will, no doubt, sweep it away with a telephone call. But it is worth a try.'

It was Saturday night, and Emily and Terry were going to the dance at the Corn Exchange. They had decided not to take Terry's new car because parking was difficult and he didn't want any passing idiot to scratch it. He had taken Emily for a short ride in it and then parked it on the road outside her flat.

There were dances on all around the town on Saturday nights, all catering for different age groups or different types of dancing. If you wanted to jive or just wave your body around a bit and you were in the age group sixteen to twenty-six, then the Corn Exchange was the place to be.

There were exceptions of course. The thirteen-year-old girls who had managed to sneak in when the doormen weren't looking and the forty-plus men, who just wouldn't face up to the fact that if they wanted to get a girl who was looking for a man nearing middle age, they needed to learn ballroom dancing.

The Corn Exchange was always crowded, inside and outside. People were arriving all the time, and others were coming out to get a drink at the pub just down the street. But the excitement it used to generate was amazing. It wasn't a pretty place. It had been fitted out to be a roller-skating rink, with barriers all around the outside of the old scuffed and dusty floor.   There was a large stage at the end opposite the entrance. The lights were low; the glitter ball was spinning. The stage stood out bright, and the live bands were loud. Every Saturday night and the atmosphere was magic.

Emily was wearing a red and black flouncy skirt and black top, that shimmered in the flashing lights. With her black high stilettos, she looked stunning. Well, that is what Terry kept telling her and, judging by the looks she was getting from the boys out on the prowl, he was right. He had a new suit on, which Emily was delighted to see was cut in the modern style. She had been encouraging him to move with the times, instead of going there in one of his accountant's suits.

They danced and danced and were both as happy as they could be. Several other boys came over and asked her for a dance, but Emily said no to them all, and Terry loved her for it. The evening seemed to fly, and it soon came to the last smooch, when the unattached made for the exit and the couples moved slowly around the floor.

Emily was beginning to see Terry in a different light. She always thought that when she found the one, the man that she could love, maybe forever, that she would know immediately it happened. But maybe that didn't work that way for everyone. Maybe you could grow to love each other, over weeks or even months.

Her thoughts were interrupted by a scuffle that seemed to be going on at the door. There was a lot of pushing and shoving. Someone was shouting obscenities at the top of his voice. But the bouncers seemed to be winning, and the ruck began to move out onto the street.

When Emily went to the cloakroom to get her coat, she asked the man behind the counter what was happening.

'Just some idiots trying to get in when we are about to close. And it turned out that they were banned in any case. About now they will will wish they hadn't tried it. All three of our doormen are ex-marines and expect people to do as they're told or else.'

'So are they well-known troublemakers?' asked Emily

'Yes, it's Billy Pope and his two idiot step brothers.'

Emily immediately went white and was rooted to the floor.

'What's the matter love. Do you know Billy Pope?' said the cloakroom man.

'Yes, she said I know who he is, but I have never seen him. I think he might be looking for me.'

Terry arrived at that point, having paid a visit the toilets while she got her coat.

Emily said quietly to Terry. 'I think we have a problem. Billy Pope is outside.'

The cloakroom ticket man was just returning coats to the last few couples to leave and then turned to Emily and Terry.

'Hang on there a minute. I'll go outside and see what's happening,' he said.

'Thank you very much, that's very nice of you,' said Emily, her voice quavering a little.

Terry added his thanks and put his arm around her shoulders.

The man returned quite quickly. He had a big grin on his face. 'It's okay; the lads have seen them off. Chased the little buggers half way down Bridge Street. They are probably still running.'

'Why is he picking on you?' he asked. 'You certainly don't look like a trouble maker to me, and you don't look like the sort of person who would go near Billy Pope.'

'It's probably because I am trying to help one of his ex-girlfriends to stand up to him. He's a real bully.' Emily didn't want to get into any further explanation. She just wanted to get home.

'How far have you got to go?' he asked.

'It's only just down Thorpe Road,' said Terry. 'Thanks ever so much for your help, but we can easily walk it.'

'The young lady looks really shook up. Tell you what,' the man said. 'I'm finished here for tonight, and my car is parked just down the road. I can easily drop you off.'

There was no stopping him now. He led them outside and introduced them to the huddle of doormen who were excitedly reliving the battle with the notorious Billy Pope and his step brothers. They turned to reassure Emily and Terry that they were safe now.

'I'm going to give them a lift home, just to make sure,' the cloakroom man said. A chorus of approval came from the doormen.

'Good idea Bert. You never know with that sneaky little bugger, he never knows when he's beaten.'

Bert led them down the road to where his car was parked. It was an immaculate little saloon, which did not surprise Emily because Bert was an immaculate little man. He held the door open for Emily and Terry to get into the back. Inside the seats were polished and everywhere looked brand new.

He walked round and got into the driver's seat.

I have never seen such a clean car,' said Emily. The smell of the polish was somehow very comforting and homely.

'I was a chauffeur for fifteen years, after the war. My boss used to meet very important people, from all over the world. He expected high standards, and I kept high standards. I am retired now. The Corn Exchange is almost a hobby for me. It keeps me in touch with music, and I love seeing the different bands. It also keeps me in touch with people, and you get all sorts here.'

Having completed his heartfelt speech, he stopped outside Emily's flat, behind Terry's newly acquired car. Bert held the door open for them.

'We can't thank you enough,' Terry said. 'Please have a drink on us.' He held the pound note out towards Bert.

He quickly turned away and said, 'No, I am not taking anything for that little ride. It's been a pleasure to meet such a nice young couple as you.'

Emily stepped forward and gave him a quick kiss on the cheek.

'Thanks, Bert,' she said. 'You are a real star.'

Bert grinned with pleasure. 'I'll have to see if I can get Billy Pope to drop in more often.'

CHAPTER 12

It was Monday morning, and Emily was sitting at her desk, thinking what a strange weekend it had been. It was funny how a shared experience of fear had somehow brought her and Terry a little closer together. Terry had suggested that they should meet up on Sunday and have a nice quiet time together, just doing nothing. Strangely, for someone who was always rushing to somewhere or from somewhere, doing nothing quite appealed to Emily. She said yes.

And the lazy Sunday just walking on the river embankment, did seem to make the incident at the Corn Exchange seem a little less real. October was only a few days away, and a cool breeze ruffled the water, giving a hint of approaching autumn. They were both glad that they had listened to Viv's advice to take their coats.

The leaves on the weeping willow trees that lined the river embankment moved restlessly, and each gust of breeze plucked a few more leaves away and scattered them along the pathway. The rowing boats that could be hired during the summer months had all been locked away in the boathouse.

Even the ice cream van had gone, and the embankment was left to a few couples clinging tightly to each other and one or two hardy families striding out purposefully.

Emily pulled herself back to the present and, for something to do, decided to clean the old black Remington typewriter, which had been allocated to her on the day she started. It probably dated back to the first world war she thought, but in use, it was excellent. However, she would give it a clean while she thought about the next move. She could see the problems, which she thought was a good starting point. All she had to do was think of a solution.

Emily was faced with the dilemma of what to do about the information that Pete had unearthed about Arnold Lackford. She decided that she would write a straightforward factual piece just covering what happened in the late 1930s between Lackford and Smithson. She would cover the pub fight, Lackford taking it to court and the court decision going to Smithson. To play safe, she put in no other material at all. No stories of later attacks on Smithson that might have been arranged by Lackford, no mention of the curtailed boxing career. These were all hearsay, so she left them out.

She rounded the story off with a version of the one discussed with Mike Townsend. This suggested that the problems between Lackford and Smithson may have been connected to the bad feeling that the two men had for each other before the war. She then went on to say that there was no reason to believe that there was any truth in these accusations, particularly as Mr Lackford was such a well-respected businessman and member of the City Council, who did a great deal of work for charity.

'Am I laying it on a bit too thick?' she asked herself. 'It is sugar coated, but people with egos like Lackford's don't tend to notice such things. I'll leave it as it is.'

Looking through the glass partition, she could see that Cadham was still not in and even if he had been there he would have been no help. She dithered for almost an hour about whether she should ring Lackford about the story. In the end, she called and spoke to Lackford's secretary. Emily asked to speak to Mr Lackford.

'What about?' The voice was sharp and aggressive.

'A story we are writing about Mr Lackford's clash with Harry Smithson, and the subsequent court case.' Emily said.

'I don't know what you are talking about. Who is Harry Smithson? I have never heard of him.' The words were spat out with venom.

'Harry Smithson is the name of the man who was murdered and washed up on a beach in Norfolk. It was in the paper last week.'

'I never read the local papers; they are just full of rubbish.'

Emily persevered. 'It was about a court case in 1939.'

'Well it's hardly news then is it? I'm not wasting Mr Lackford's time with that.' And the phone went dead.

Emily sat and thought about her next move. She decided that she would submit the story and see what happened. Then she thought again and decided to do a very short piece just along the lines that she had agreed with DCI Thompson. It was a lot shorter than the other piece, and that was usually a good thing. Then she had another change of mind, and she tore them both up and did a shorter version of the whole story from before the war, after the war and to the present time – 1961.

She read it through again and was just about to take it to the sub-editors when Betty, the editor's secretary came bustling down the corridor.

'Are you working on a story about Arnold Lackford?' she asked breathlessly. Emily looked puzzled and handed it to Betty.

Betty scanned it quickly with a practised eye and went quite white.

She began to walk away, while saying over her shoulder. 'Don't do anything else on this and don't ring Lackford again.'

Emily sat with her head in her hands. What had she done wrong? They hadn't even read her story, and it contained nothing that had not been published before. It looked as though Lackford had made a call to someone at the paper to get it dropped. If so, was that the action of an innocent man?

Maybe it was. It would not be the first time that a newspaper story had ruined someone's reputation, but the answer to that is don't do things that will come back to haunt you in later life. His treatment of Harry Smithson deserved some retribution. She was giving him the chance to tell his side of the story. If he had nothing to hide, why not come forward and say so.

Emily felt the annoyance rising inside her. She was not at her best in this sort of mood and the quicker she got out of the way, the better it would be. Grabbing her handbag and notebook, she stood up and hurried to the door. She was through reception and out the door in seconds. Fortunately, the receptionist was dealing with two people at the desk. Otherwise she would have had to stop for a short chat. She always did, so It would be expected.

She walked to the small line of red telephone kiosks, near the old Guild Hall and next to the police station. She went into the first and opened her notebook. At the very back, she kept a list of telephone numbers that related to this story.

First, she rang DCI Mike Townsend. She knew that he was probably only sitting about twenty yards away in his office. She also knew that Mike Townsend would prefer her not go into the police station.

Working together would be frowned upon by his colleagues.

A female voice answered.

'Could I speak to DCI Townsend please?' Emily asked.

'Who is it calling please?'

'Emily Miller. He will know what it's about,' Emily said, anticipating what the next question would be.

'Oh, okay, I'll put you through then,' she said as if she was sure he would not take the call.

'Hello,' he said cheerfully. 'What have you got to tell me?'

'I wrote the story, as we discussed and a dozen other versions as well. I gave Lackford a chance to put his side of the story, and within minutes the editor's secretary was snatching it off my desk and telling me not to call him again.'

'Well,' said Mike happily, 'I think you have stirred the hornets' nest very nicely. I was hoping we might get a reaction like that. I think it would be well worth leaving this to us now. We don't want to get you into more trouble.'

'Yes, I had to come out to cool down. I knew I was close to saying something I shouldn't. Everybody seems to be against me at the moment.'

'Could I ask a favour please,' he said. 'Could you get copies of the newspaper stories that you used when you wrote the piece on Lackford. I checked the files we have here, but they are not complete, and I would like to have as much as possible with me when we go to speak to him.'

'Yes, of course, how should I get them to you?'

'I could meet you in that coffee shop in Cumbergate, just around the corner from the Post Office,' he said. 'About four this afternoon?'

'Yes, I'll be there.'

Next was a call to Geoff Upthorne. Emily rooted around in her bag for some loose change and then dialled. The phone rang for quite a while, but eventually, he answered. Emily told him what had happened and asked what she should do next.

'Mm, I can guess what is going on. I don't know him personally, but I know what sort of man he is,' he said. 'He will honestly believe that he is untouchable. Way above the law that ordinary people have to live by. He will feel that he has everyone in his pocket – press, police, and everyone else that matters.

'In his young days, he did it by brute force, but he soon learned that controlling people that way wasn't easy. There were always bigger, stronger men ready to take him on.'

'So, what did he do?' asked Emily.

'He sought out people with power and made friends with them. By then, thanks to the war, he had made enough money to share the lifestyle that those sorts of people enjoy. He has used his money to cement these friendships by investing in their projects or businesses, by being a high-profile contributor to good causes and generally buying himself respectability.

'I am afraid your story has run into a problem that all newspapers suffer from time to time. It is a straightforward dilemma. What do you do when a story shows one of your biggest advertisers in a bad light. I faced it myself. And I am afraid the answer is, you drop the story.'

Emily was speechless for a moment but then said. 'Is that really the case?'

'Yes, it's a fact of life. But don't worry, most journalists who have this happen to them feel the same as you. I did the first time it happened to me. But the story will get out one way or another. In the nationals maybe, or just by word of mouth. You would be amazed how quickly damaging news can get around.'

'So you don't think I am in trouble at work?'

'No. This is something that any journalist hates. But the facts are that without advertising, newspapers would struggle financially. I know what it is like and the word would have come down from on high. And that would be that. No argument.'

'So you think I will be safe to go back,' Emily said, with a nervous laugh. 'I've been hiding in this telephone box for about twenty minutes now.'

'Honestly, everyone will be quite embarrassed that they have had to ditch the story. They ought to have explained this to you, but I guess there was a bit of panic going on. There usually is.'

'I have told Mike, and he wants me to let him have the material we got from the back issues. He says, with what they have in their files, he would have enough to go and question Lackford.'

'That's very good to hear. Mike will do it very well. He will be very low key and play the It's just routine card. But he will be watching Lackford and will know if he is lying.

Emily felt a lot better after that. She walked back to the office. Nobody was looking at her, and no one came to speak to her, so she carried on as normal. She had two copies of the material about Lackford, so she separated them and put one set in a large brown envelope.

At five to four she set off from the office towards the coffee house where she was to meet Mike Townsend. As soon as she stepped into the crowded little shop, she saw Mike. He looked at her and inclined his head in the direction of the table at the back right-hand corner. Emily immediately saw that there were two reporters from the paper sitting at the table. She had been introduced, but she could not recall their names. This was one of the problems of not working in the same room as the other journalist. She thought that one was sports editor and the other she couldn't remember, maybe motoring.

She instantly recognised that Mike was letting her know that he did not want her to go to his table while they were sitting there. Emily quickly looked around the room and then at the small queue gathered at the counter. Then she looked at her watch, turned and walk out as if she hadn't got time to wait. She crossed the road and walked slowly towards St Johns Church, just looking back occasionally.

About three minutes later Mike Townsend exited the coffee shop and walked towards her.

'Let's go down here,' he said, and they walked towards the railway station. 'I'm glad you spotted those two in the corner. They came in just after I arrived, so I couldn't just get up and leave. I know it doesn't really matter, but I would rather keep our working relationship to ourselves and avoid the inevitable sniping. Helping each other like this usually works well, but we need to trust each other completely. When things do go wrong, and they occasionally do, you must be able to rely on one another to do the right thing.'

'Yes, I understand that, but as I'm only a novice in this business I hope you don't mind me checking with you when I am not sure if I am doing the right thing.'

'No, call me whenever you are in doubt. That way we at least know what is likely to happen next.'

As they walked along, she passed him the brown envelope, and he rolled it up and stuck it in his coat pocket.

'I have talked it through with my team,' he said, 'and we feel that we are fully justified in asking Lackford a few questions about what he was doing in and around the time that Harry Smithson was demobbed. If it was anyone else we wouldn't hesitate, so why not extend the privilege to the high and mighty Arnold Lackford.

The following day Geoff Upthorne called Emily at work and said he had a new lead for her. He said he would pick her up from the newspaper office at 12.30 and take her to lunch. Emily left the office a few minutes early so that she wouldn't keep him waiting. He arrived on time and drove her to a nice, quiet pub on the outskirts of town.

They ordered two halves of bitter and two ploughmen's and sat in a distant corner of the pub so that no one could overhear anything.

'After your call about Lackford, I started thinking if I had anything in my old notebooks about Smithson, Pope or Lackford. It was a long shot because I have never had a great memory, but I do write everything possible down in my notes. I thought that they might be useful someday. You never know, I may want to write my memoirs.'

'You should,' said Emily. 'It would be a great insight for young journalists like me, trying to learn the business.'

'One day maybe,' he said. 'At the moment, I have more than enough to do.'

'Like getting up into the attic trying to find a clue to a fourteen-year-old murder,' Emily smiled.

'Well I know which is more interesting and it's not my memoirs.' he said, taking several sheets of paper from his pocket.

'I decided to look back, right from 1945,' he said. 'They were kept in date order, and I had a habit of underlining names because they were what I always forgot, and still do for that matter. I can usually remember what happened, but not the names involved.

'I went through them all reasonably quickly, because so many of the stories were nothing to do with any crimes. For crime stories, I underlined the headings in red.'

Emily had to smile to herself at the meticulous discipline he must have had to keep the system going all those years. It made her somewhat chaotic note-taking and haphazard filing system seem a little amateurish. She made a mental note to review it and start over again.

'Anyway,' Geoff continued, 'there was one name that cropped up several times, particularly in relation to incidents and the court case involving Smithson and Lackford. The name is Walter Green. He seems to have been an acquaintance and possibly a friend of Smithson. I also have an address for him. I know it is almost thirty years ago, but it is in deepest fenland. Often houses in the fens are just passed on from generation to generation, and people just don't move away from the area. I think it must be that so much employment comes from the land that its best to stay where the work is.'

Emily nodded agreement and could not hide her delight at having another lead to follow. It meant that her investigation could continue at the same time as the police enquiry. It was another line to follow, and she had been feeling quite down about having nothing to follow up. This crime reporting was like a drug, and she had to admit that she was well and truly hooked.

'Thank you for that Geoff; I was getting frustrated at not being able to follow up on all the information. It is really good of you.'

He smiled. 'I know how you must have been feeling. It's just how I would have felt. And after all, I had said about what a wonderful career journalism is, it seemed that this was just a big let-down. So, I hope this has restored a little faith.'

'It has, and I'll go to see Walter Green tomorrow.'

'Is there anyone who can go with you?' he asked.

'Not unless John Cadham is back at work? And in any case, I will be very careful and make it clear to Green that people know I have come to see him.'

'Okay, you do that. I have no reason to believe that he is trouble. Nothing in my notes suggested he was anything but a decent bloke, ready to stand up for a friend.'

CHAPTER 13

As expected, there was no sign of John Cadham at work the next morning. Emily was pleased really. Yes, she would have felt safer to have someone with her, but Cadham's constant negativity and scepticism were more than she could stand. And he would inevitably upset Green and cause him to clam up.

She borrowed a large-scale map from Pete and spoke to Jim, the delivery driver who had been on the receiving end of Lackford's punch in the pub. Jim was a fen-lander himself, who had now moved to Whittlesey, a small town near Peterborough. Jim knew the area where Walter Green lived and went through the directions on the map. He gave Emily some useful landmarks to look out for so that she could be sure she was on the right road.

Emily took the little Ford Anglia from the car pool and set off in the direction of Wisbech. She had the map next to her on the front passenger seat and her notebook open, with a list of landmarks that Jim had given her. As there are very few actual landmarks in the fens, the list she had made was like a series of clues to guide her. It included a red tractor with no wheels, a dead tree that had split in half, two rusty cars and an old boat decaying in a front garden. Emily smiled to herself. It was like a motoring treasure hunt, similar to those her hockey club in St Albans used to organise to raise funds.

She drove carefully through the little village of Eye and on towards the bigger village of Thorney, with its remains of an old Abbey signposted on the main road. The day was cold, but the sun shone brightly, and Emily was amazed at the flatness of the landscape. She seemed to be able to see for miles and miles. The white clouds were being blown along by a stiff breeze in a pure blue sky. To Emily's surprise, it made a magnificent sight. The huge sky seemed to reduce everything at ground level to miniatures. Tiny tractors that must have been nearly a half a mile away could be seen ploughing the rich black earth. A lone tree in a field looked like a bonsai plant.

After she had passed through Thorney, she came to an even longer straight road, which Jim had told her was appropriately called the Guyhirn Straight. Just before she reached Guyhirn, Jim had told her to turn left. But as she didn't know how far she was from Guyhirn, she went too far and had to turn around in the village.

After that, the instructions worked very well. She saw the red tractor with no wheels, parked next to a dilapidated old barn and turned left after a quarter of a mile. The two rusting cars, with one, laid neatly on top of the other, meant that she should make a right turn in a mile.

The roads now were down to a single track, with grass verges providing a small margin between the road and a steeply banked drainage ditch. There was a feeling of desolation and roads that seemed to be going nowhere. Emily, a lifetime town girl, felt very lost and disconcerted. She almost considered turning back. Then she saw the house with, what looked like a dilapidated old ships lifeboat, sitting on the front lawn. Someone had filled it with soil and planted flowers in it. Almost immediately, Emily saw two semi-detached houses, standing in isolation at the end of a dirt track. It was just as Jim had described. This was where Walter Green lived.

Emily drove slowly down the driveway, carefully avoiding the biggest potholes, and looked intently ahead at the two little cottages. Neither had numbers on the doors. The cottage on the left looked the better kept, with much cleaner curtains in the windows. Emily guessed that the one on the right would be Walter's. And she guessed right.

After two knocks on the door, she heard movement inside. The door opened slowly, and a man in baggy grey trousers, braces and a shirt that had once been white stood, looking bewildered.

'I am looking for Walter Green,' Emily said.

Yes, that's me,' he said nervously. 'What do you want?'

'It's nothing to worry about Mr Green. Sorry if I disturbed you. My name is Emily, and I just wanted to talk to you about Harry Smithson. I believe you were a friend of his?' She held her card out for him to look at, but he did not take his eyes off her.

'You'd better come in. The place is a mess. I haven't had a chance to clear up,' he grumbled to himself as he limped back to a threadbare armchair, standing next to an unlit fireplace. He dropped into the armchair and waved Emily to sit in the armchair opposite. A black and white cat was lying on a newspaper on the chair. The cat looked sleepily at Emily as if daring her to try sitting there. Emily glanced around at alternatives, but the two other seats in the room were piled high with clothes, papers, books and assorted other rubbish.

Emily took a step towards the cat, and it leapt from the chair and rushed out through the door. At that moment, Emily would have loved to have followed it. She removed the newspaper from the chair. It was folded so that the racing pages were on the outside and Walter had been ticking his selections. She sat down and took out her notebook, thinking she was pleased that she had chosen to wear her dark jeans today.

'Thank you for talking to me,' Emily began. 'I'm from the newspaper in Peterborough. We've been working on a story about the Harry Smithson murder, and I understand that you knew him quite well before the war.'

'Yes, I knew him. He was a good old boy, was Harry. Big lad. I always felt safe when he was around. You could trust him, so I sort of hung around with him.'

'Can you think of anyone from that time who might have wanted to kill him?'

Walter looked troubled. 'Are you really from the newspaper? Don't seem right, a little old gal, asking questions like that.'

Emily smiled. She liked people who said what they were thinking, and Walter was plainly baffled by her appearance. 'I'm older than I look.' She gave him the stock answer.

She decided to try another approach. 'Do you know Billy Pope or Arnold Lackford?'

'Yes, I know them, most people do around here. Why do you want to know?'

'They are just names that have cropped up in my investigation. Do you have any idea who might have wanted Harry Smithson out the of the way?' she asked.

'Yes, I do as it happens, but it would be the end of me if I told you. I'm not completely daft you know?' The effort of speaking brought on a coughing fit, which went on for a while.'

After he had calmed down, Emily asked, 'Who are you protecting?'

'I'm protecting myself, 'Green said. 'I'm dying you know.' He paused to get his breath again. 'I have to be careful. I've got TB. Had it for years. It's slowly getting worse year by year. But I know that I don't have much time left. I've got to do the right thing sometime. I got to face up to what I done'

Shocked at what Green had said, Emily was lost for words for a moment. Then she said, 'I am so sorry to hear that Mr Green. What do you mean, you have to do the right thing?'

'Yes, well. That's how it is. I've got to face reality. I have been carrying this secret for so long. I must set the record straight. And I will. This is what I was trying to do when I told what had happened to Harry that night in the pub. I did a terrible thing. There were two of us that did it. There is not a day goes by that I haven't thought about it since. Not an hour. It was over twenty years ago now. But it still hangs over me like a black cloud.'

He fell silent, and then there was only the whisper of the breeze to be heard, sweeping across the open fields and over the little house.

'What was the secret you shared with Harry that night in the pub?' She asked quietly.

'It was that little old pub on the main road. It ain't there now. Turned it into a house, they did. It was popular because the beer was cheap and it was a good place to meet up with blokes from all around this area. Pity it's gone now.' Walter seemed to be talking to himself.

'We had a bit to drink. Well, I'd had plenty. I felt that if I told someone about what had happened, it might not feel so bad and it might not keep coming back to me day after day, night after night. You know what they say about a trouble shared. Well, it doesn't work. When the trouble is so bad that you just can't stop thinking about it, nothing can make you feel any better.

'Harry kept saying he didn't want to know what I'd done. And he didn't want to know who was with me. But I kept on and on. I just had to get it off my chest. Told him who it was. Who planned it all. Who made me go with him and do it.

'I told Harry why I had to help. He had helped me out so many times, with money and other things. He was always there for me, and now I owed it to him to help, but I didn't know what was going to happen. If I'd have known I would never have gone with him.'

Walter's story just tailed off, and Emily sat in silence, hoping he would give her the name that she needed to solve the murder.

Eventually, he began again, but now he was quietly saying the words and Emily had to lean forward to hear.

'It was a terrible thing we did, and we should have paid the price. But the strange thing was that after I had told Harry the secret. I felt that I had betrayed another trust. The man who had helped me all those times and had put his trust in me to do the job with him. I felt so bad when I sobered up that I told him what I had done.

'He was furious at first, but then he calmed down and said he could fix it. It would be okay. I didn't know what that meant, but then I heard that Harry had been called up and was gone to the war. I thought that would be the end of it, and it was until the other day when someone told me that Harry Smithson might have been murdered. They said they had seen it in the paper. They said it had happened fourteen years ago and I knew straight away who had done it. It had to be him.'

'And are you willing to give me that name?' asked Emily. 'I promise you that the police will protect you.'

'He's too smart for the police. He would find a way of getting to me.'

'Please give me a name, and I will keep it a secret until the police arrest him.'

'You don't know what he's like. I will tell you,' said Green, 'but not right now. He would kill me. I know he would, and I know I don't have much time left, but when you are dying every day matters.'

Emily was not going to argue with that. She looked at Walter, slumped in his chair and looking exhausted after reliving the horrors of his life.

'I understand,' she said. 'I am sorry that I have upset you and made you remember all that. Can we keep in touch? It is important that we find the murderer.'

I will make sure that I do the right thing, I promise,' he said. 'I will give the name to you and do the right thing.'

'Can I get you anything before I go. I could make you a cup of tea.' She offered.

'No, Elsie from next door will come round after you've gone. She looks after me when she can, and she'll want to know who you were.'

Emily drove back on the long straight roads from Guyhirn. Her head was still spinning from what Walter Green had said. Who was this other man? What did they do? Did this mystery man kill Harry? What is Walter's big secret?

He is a pathetic man, but underneath she thought he was also a good man. He'd got himself tied up with something he couldn't handle, and it had virtually ruined his life.

CHAPTER 14

When Emily arrived at work, there was a note on her desk saying that John Cadham had called to say that he was coming in today, but he might be a little late. So what's new, thought Emily. She went to update Pete on what had happened at Walter Green's house and then dropped in to thank Jim for his excellent directions.

Cadham eventually arrived at 2.45 in the afternoon. Emily could hear the banter flying as he waddled to his desk grinning. She could see from where she was sitting that he still had a black eye and his right arm appeared to be in a sling.

Emily thought she'd better do the decent thing and see how he was getting on.

She walked through to his desk. Up close, he still had several cuts and bruises on his face. He obviously had been drinking. His words were very slightly slurred, and he had a fixed grin on his face, which he always used after coming back from a liquid lunch. He must think it makes him look sober, thought Emily, but in fact it makes him look as if he was about to say something, but has forgotten what is was.

'I'm really sorry what happened John,' she said.

'Yes, I bet you are,' he replied.

'It must have been a case of mistaken identity,' she said with a smile.

'It wasn't bloody funny,' he said. 'I could have been killed.'

'I never said it was funny,' she replied. 'It's just that I think they thought that someone else had written the article until they saw the by-line.'

Cadham glared at Emily. 'It's OK, I put the bastards who were trying to kill me right about that,' he said bitterly.

'Oh, thanks,' she said. 'So now Billy Pope is looking for me again. Did you tell the police that you said it was me?'

'I might have done. I can't remember. I can give them a ring.'

'Don't worry, I'll give them a call,' she said, thinking it was time to change the subject before for she lost her temper.'

'We have another suspect and another good lead. I went to see a man called Walter Green, in the fens near Guyhirn,' she said.

'I don't want to hear anything about it, not a bloody word.' Cadham shouted. It was as if the fear and shock within him had suddenly manifested itself in that one sentence. The whole office turned to look at them. 'I don't want to hear anything,' he said, shouting even louder. 'Just keep it away from me. I don't want to hear it. I don't want to hear anything from you, you little bitch.'

Emily picked up the pile of information she was going to show him and looked around for someone else to say something. One of the other senior reporters stood up and came over to where Cadham sat, slumped over his desk.

He put his hand on Cadham's shoulder. 'Come on John my old mate. I think you've come back too soon, I'll give you a lift home, and you take it easy.'

He waited for Cadham to get himself together and then led him towards the door. Emily went back to her desk.

When the reporter returned from taking John home, he stopped by Emily's desk.

'I think he is very shaken up still, and he's probably been off the booze for a while, especially while he was in hospital. He'll be back large as life and twice as obnoxious. But I think you have got the measure of him. The names Steve by the way. If you need any help, you know where I am.'

'Thanks,' said Emily. 'I'll do that.'

She hadn't expected Cadham's return to be so dramatic or so short lived. She was hoping that running through the new information she had would enable her to decide what to do next. She had found in the past, that when she had something complex to work out, the best thing was to stop thinking about it and do something to take your mind off the problem.

Go to the pictures, she thought. She dropped into the ad sales office and saw Viv.

'Do you fancy going to the pictures tonight?' Emily asked Viv.

'Yes, I'm game. What's on?'

Emily had already checked. 'Breakfast at Tiffany's.'

'They say it's a lovely film and Audrey Hepburn's dresses are fabulous.' Viv said.

'Shall we go straight after work? Just get a snack at the KitKat. It's on at the City Cinema'

'Yes, that's great. There is nothing like a surprise trip to the flicks. See you in about an hour then,' said Viv.

Viv and Emily enjoyed their visit to the cinema. The film had made them laugh and even cry, just a little, and Emily enjoyed watching Audrey Hepburn. That was who she wanted to be like. A woman who could look just as good in jeans and a jumper as she did in a beautiful evening dress. A woman who could be both vulnerable and strong at the same time.

Emily left the cinema with her head full of images of beautiful people, amazing New York and the story of a girl who wanted to make a good life for herself. As she walked with Viv along the pavement in Bridge Street, they were both silent, almost as if they did not want to break the magic spell created by the film.

Then, suddenly Emily was aware of heavy footsteps behind them. People on the crowded pavement were being jostled and pushed, by someone that she could not see properly, then suddenly she saw what it was. One man is pushing the people who were leaving the cinema out of the way. Then she saw two bigger men lumbering along behind. She knew at once that it was Billy Pope and his step brothers.

People were shouting in protest at being manhandled but were so startled they could not react to what was happening. Emily reacted instinctively and took off running, shouting at Viv to run as well.

But Viv was wearing her high heels, and running was just not a practical option. Also, she had no idea why Emily had taken off as if her life depended on it. Then the three men rushed past her, and she realised that they were not interested in her. Emily was the one they were after.

Emily's burst of speed had taken her some way ahead of the chasing pack, but she did not think that she could keep her sprint up for very long. The traffic was light at that time of the evening, so she ran across the road, weaving between a small car and a cyclist. Then, when she reached the marketplace, on an impulse, she turned right, into the Cathedral precincts.

She hoped that she was so far ahead and that Billy Pope and his thugs had not seen where she had gone. It was very much darker in the precincts, with just a few ancient lampposts, placed at the corners of the three large lawns in front of the West Front of the Cathedral. The light they produced was an eerie glow across the precincts. It created a feeling that she had suddenly gone back in time, to a darker, more violent age. The burst of adrenaline that had propelled her down Bridge Street was nearly all used up now, and Emily knew that she had to think and act quickly if she was going to avoid the same fate that John Cadham had experienced.

She was walking quickly and turned left onto the pavement that served the row of three-story townhouses, leading to the North gate of the precincts. This, in turn, led to Wheelers Yard, the small road that cuts through to Midgate. At that moment, she heard the clatter of boots on the cobbled road behind her.

She started to run again, only to find that the gate was locked at night. She turned and saw the three men standing near the first lamp post, looking around. She quickly opened the iron gate leading to one of the houses. The small front garden, had steps leading up to the main door, with letterbox, number and a bell push. Immediately to the left were some steps leading down to a basement.

There was a faint glow of light from the large window, next to the front door, but the steps leading downwards were almost in complete darkness. Emily felt her way carefully down the steps into the darkness. She felt strangely calm, but at the same time, she could feel her heart pumping at the sudden rush of activity that had brought her here.

She could hear the men talking to each other. They seem to be spreading out in their search for her, and some of the voices got louder.

'She can't have gone far,' a far off deep voice called. 'Should I have a look down here?'

'Where does it lead to?' a lighter voice.

'I don't know.'

'Well go and have a bloody look then, you stupid sod.' The lighter, but hard voice again, Emily thought. He sounds in charge, it must be Billy Pope.

'It's bloody dark round here,' A voice called from a distance. 'No old gal would go down here. She'd be pissing herself. Fucking hell, there are gravestones, all over the place.'

'What do you expect, it's a fucking church isn't it,' said the voice from nearby.

Emily froze. The voice was just above her. She slowly sank onto the bottom step. Pulling her knees up to her chin and wrapping her arms around her legs. Emily could make herself very small, she had done it before, and it worked then. But this time it had to work, or she was in big trouble.

The first time was when she hid in the cupboard under the stairs at home. That was when she discovered how small she could make herself. She was playing hide and seek with her cousins, a boy, and a girl a little older than her. They couldn't find her, and she felt so safe and secure in the dark cupboard, she wouldn't give up her hiding place. Her mother and father joined in the hunt and were getting increasingly distressed, so she opened the door and came out smiling triumphantly.

She got the telling-off of her life and hide and seek was banned from the house. They couldn't believe how she fitted herself into such a small space. Now she was having to use the same trick again, and there would be no second chances if they found her.

Her bottom seemed to be sitting on something very wet and slimy. She felt with her hand. It was a layer of wet, rotting leaves that had fallen off the bushes. She was relieved, it could have been something much worse than a few damp leaves.

'I'm going to check this gate.' The voice was right over the top of her now. She looked up but could see no one. That meant he probably couldn't see her. But she could hear him breathing. She lowered her head and held her breath.

'The gates locked. She couldn't get out this way,' he shouted. 'I'll come back to you after I've checked these gardens.'

Emily realised that these gardens must include the one she was hiding in. There was only two to check before he would find her. Could I get up the stairs and then run off again, she thought. She quickly weighed up the possibility of escaping. She felt sure she could outrun Billy, but she had to get past him at the gate, and as soon as she started to climb the steps to ground level he would hear her. She knew he would catch her before she had a chance to run. And she was sure he would have a knife. That was Billy Pope's chosen weapon.

He checked the first garden quickly. Just a cursory glance. 'Nothing in that one,' he called to no one in particular.

There might be a chance he could miss her in the darkness, but as her eyes had become accustomed to the dark, she could see the small garden around her quite clearly. She heard his boots grating on the stone steps next door. She shivered in the cold fear that he was so close now and she felt sure he would have the knife ready in his hand. He had sounded quite nervous when he last spoke, and Emily thought he might be getting spooked by the surroundings and semi-darkness in the precincts.

From where she was sitting, she started to feel around the small garden for a make-do weapon of some sort that she could hit him with as he came down the steps. Her hand touched metal. She traced the shape of the object with her hand. I was a small metal bucket, filled with small stones and weeds. Someone had been tidying up the garden and had left the bucket outside. She gently lifted the handle and began to test the weight of the bucket and its contents.

Then she heard the scrape of boots on the pavement. He was at the gate to the garden that she was hiding in. She heard the groan of the iron hinges on the gate above her. She sensed that the man she guessed was Billy Pope was now inside the gate. She couldn't just sit there and wait to see what happened. She had to do something to defend herself.

She stood up quickly and turned to face him. Her eyes were adjusted to the near darkness, and she saw him step back in surprise. He probably couldn't see her very clearly at the bottom of the steps, but that was no advantage because she was now completely trapped. He stood directly between her and the escape route into the precincts. He moved forward slightly, and she saw the glint of what she knew was the blade of a knife.

'Got you, you bitch,' he snarled. 'You are going to wish that you hadn't written that shit about me in the paper.'

Emily said nothing. At that moment, she was frozen with fear. To say anything was an impossibility. She felt like an animal trapped in a cage.

He moved forward and started to go slowly down the steps on which she had been sitting. She could see his arm held out in front of him and the blade pointed towards her. She backed slowly away into the darkness but felt a bush behind her that prevented her from going any further.

She stopped, but then realised that she was still holding the bucket with the stones and garden rubbish in it. Her fingers were wrapped tightly around the bucket handle as it hung by her side. As he moved forward, she swung the bucket back and then forward. She let go of the handle, and the bucket flew towards him. It had gathered considerable momentum and seemed to hit him round about the knee area, or maybe a little higher.

It stopped him in his tracks and knocked him off balance.

'You fucking bitch,' he screamed at her. 'You're going to pay for that.'

Emily turned and scrambled over the bush and a small rockery. She wasn't thinking properly, but some instinct of self-preservation had kicked in, and she found herself trying to climb the wall to the next garden.

She had just clambered up to the top of the wall and was expecting Billy Pope to pull her back down when she heard the sound of police whistles and people shouting.

She heard him scrambling back up the steps and then the grating of his boots as he started to run on the cobblestones. His feet are fighting to get some grip on the ground.

'Get out, get out,' he shouted at the top of his voice as he ran.

There was more shouting and more whistles sounding. Emily climbed down into the garden again and then move slowly up the stone steps, keeping her body close to the ground. Peeping over the top of the highest step she saw a running man turn left past the big house on the corner and headed towards the road that ran to the left of the Cathedral and led to other houses at the back.

'There's one of them.' She heard the shout go up.

'You can get him. Try and cut him off at the arch.'

Emily kept low to the ground and waited. She wasn't sure if they had all gone or not. One of them could have hidden, waiting for her to come out. Then she heard the voice of Viv calling to her.

'Emily. Are you there? It's safe now. You can come out. The police are here.'

Emily climbed unsteadily out from her cold, damp hiding place. She was shaking all over, she was cold, her jeans were all wet, but a wave of euphoria took hold of her, and she began to laugh. Then she saw Viv and ran to her, and they both began to cry.

'I went to fetch help from the police station, said Viv through her tears. It was so close I thought it was better than me trying to stop them.'

'Yes, it was, and you were only just in time. Thank you, Viv. You saved me' Then they both cried again.

The police continued to search, but Billy and his step brothers seemed to have slipped away in the darkness of the precincts.

Viv and Emily went to the police station and made statements about what had happened. The police then drove them back to their flat. The Constable who drove them home said they were already out patrolling the town and setting up road blocks.

He offered to take the girls to have a check-up at the hospital, but they just wanted to get home and said they were OK. He warned them that shock can be delayed and they might not feel the effects for an hour or two. Brandy would help them to calm down, he recommended. It sounded like good advice to Viv and Emily, but as they had no brandy, the girls thought a few shots of Vodka might do the job just as well.

CHAPTER 15

The next morning, she walked to work with Viv. They felt safer together. There was no sign of anyone watching them.

When they arrived at the office, Emily immediately called the police station to ask if Billy Pope had been caught. She was asked to stay on the line while they checked. After a few moments delay, the familiar voice of Mike Townsend came on the line.

'Hello, how are you and your friend?' he asked, with real concern in his voice.

'Oh, we're okay. Still, a bit shocked I think. But we were well looked after at the station last night.'

'That's good to hear. We are all very disappointed that we couldn't catch them. They must have had help from someone very close to the town centre because we had all roads out sealed off. We're now going door to door in selected parts of the town because we think they could be holed up somewhere.'

'I was going to check that Janet was OK,' Emily said. 'You know Billy Pope's ex-girlfriend.

'She thought he might have come back from Ireland in 1946 to take Harry Smithson off the scene. I was wondering if she had heard anything from him now he has returned. But I feel sure she would have let me know if she had.'

'I don't think he has been anywhere near her flat. We have been keeping an eye on her in case he showed up again. If she suspected anything, I think she would have told us.' Townsend said.

'I was going to go round there this morning to make sure that she was okay?' she said.

'That is one of the places our team are checking on. Wait until I give you the all clear. That could well be the sort of place they would go to and force their way inside. We don't want you walking into that.'

'Okay, I'll wait to hear from you,' she said. 'Don't forget there is the other girl, Julie, in the downstairs flat with her baby. She knows Pope too.'

He promised to remind the team and then rang off.

She looked through the glass panel and saw that Cadham was not at his desk, but Steve was there. He was the reporter who had helped when Cadham had his meltdown the other day.

She walked through to Steve's desk.

'Good morning Steve,' she said with a smile, 'any news from John?'

'Not from him, no, but I understand he has been given some extended leave to get over the attack and, between you and me, the drinking problem.' He said the last three words in a semi-whisper and exaggerated lip movements.

'Oh, I see, so I wonder who I report to now.'

'Whoever you want I should think. Haven't you noticed how the paper functions? I think they call it light touch management. If you know a job needs doing, you do it. Don't ask, just do it. It sounds crazy I know, but it seems to work.'

Emily didn't know whether to believe him or not. 'Are you serious?'

'Yes, I don't know if they do it on purpose, but that is how it works. So, who do you want to report to?'

'Well, as you are the only other person I know, apart from Pete. I think I will choose you.'

'A very good choice, if I may say so. All the stuff for John has been left on his desk, and I have been checking for anything urgent. There hasn't been anything that can't wait for a couple of days, so everything that is there now you can have all to yourself.

'And furthermore, since you have, all on your own, managed to get rid of, the bane of our lives, John Cadham, you can have this desk here to work on.' He smacked his hand down on the top of the desk that stood between Cadham's desk and his.'

Emily could not stop smiling. 'But I was told there was no room for me?'

'Ah, John would say that because he is petrified of women. Whenever he gets into an argument with a woman, he comes off second best. And he knew as soon as he saw you, who was going to be the boss. And like a lemming drawn to the cliff edge, he just couldn't stop himself pressing the button marked humiliation. And if you sit there it will make it one of the most improved views in the history of mankind.'

'You're just teasing me,' Emily said, suddenly serious.

'Only about the way the paper is run and that you could choose who to report to, he laughed. When you came in, I had only just come out of Martin Yates' office. He had told me what the changes were to be and that I should tell you. You couldn't have come at a more opportune moment.'

'That was unkind,' she said, but she still smiled happily.

'And the editor, Martin Yates, actually told you I could move in here. I thought he had forgotten about me.'

'No, of course not. He keeps calling you the new girl, so I reminded him that you had been here for a year now.'

'And what did he say to that?' she asked.

'He wrote it down on the list that he keeps on his desk. I can guarantee that when you do go to see him, he will call you by one of the names on his list. It might not be yours, but it will be one from the list.'

'That's very comforting,' she said, looking around the newsroom. 'I can only see two other girls, so at least there is a one in three chance that he will get the right one.'

Steve laughed. 'Go fetch your goods and chattels, my good woman; we have work to do.'

Emily went off to get her things. I am going to enjoy working here, she thought, but the trauma of last night still hung over her. She noticed that her hands were shaking as she collected her things together and every little noise in the office seemed to make her jump.

The police called Emily at around half past two and said that they had checked on Janet and Julie and everything was alright. They had not seen or heard anything from Billy Pope and had satisfied themselves the men were not hiding anywhere on the premises, or in the garden.

Emily decided that she would not go to see them because it might seem that they were still in danger. She realised that she was the one in the firing line now and the less Janet and Julie knew about what was happening, the better.

She moved her stuff into the newsroom and decided to get Steve up to speed with what had happened so far.

She gathered all the information they had accumulated over the last few weeks, and she and Steve moved to a small conference room to go through it all.

Steve was a very good listener. He only interrupted her when he didn't understand something and occasionally took notes. He let her get to the end, before giving his opinion. He did look slightly surprised that Emily was working with the police but immediately saw the necessity when working a case like this. He also agreed to keep the information between the two of them.

'That is some story. I guess that fourteen-year-old murders are never going to be simple. What is your gut feeling about the suspects you have so far? To me, speaking as a journalist, Arnold Lackford would make the best story, but Billy Pope is probably the most likely villain.'

'Yes, I agree completely. I don't see Lackford throwing away what he had built-up during the war, on a stupid vendetta. He had made a fool of himself once, but people like him always draw the line when the likelihood of losing money shows itself.'

'So, what about this Green character? What do you think he knows?'

Emily paused to think and then said, 'I really believe he knows who killed Smithson. What I don't know is whether it was Pope, Lackford or someone else.'

'What do you think we should do next?' Steve said. 'Do you think that if we both went to see this Green fellow, we could get a bit more out of him.'

'Yes, it is possible. He is a very frightened man. And with good reason. He's dying from TB, and he is frightened to death about naming the murderer. I pressed him as hard as I could,' she paused. 'Well no, I pressed him as hard as I was willing to. I felt really sorry for him.'

'I never faced a situation quite like that, but I can imagine what it felt like. Promise me that you won't go to see Green on your own in the future.

'Martin Yates did say to me that I shouldn't let you go to interview people like Green on your own. He can't believe that Cadham was letting you put yourself in danger like he did,' Steve said.

'Well, it wasn't always him. There was the Corn Exchange and my trip to the pictures last night,' she said.

'Yes, heard about that. I was surprised when I saw you walk in this morning. That sort of shock can take days to get over. You are a real fighter, aren't you Emily? But sometimes you can be too brave for your own good,' Steve said.

He continued, 'I am sure you are going to be careful until this story is sorted out, but when you need to go out and interview these dodgy characters, I am going to be with you. It's still your story, but you've got some back-up now.'

'Believe me, I'm not really brave,' she said. 'And I'm not desperate for it to be my story. I constantly have to ask people for advice because I'm new to this. I'd much prefer it to be our story and for us to see it through from now onwards.'

Steve smiled. 'You've got a deal. We can crack this one, no matter how difficult it is.'

For the first time in the last two weeks, Emily walked home with Viv without thinking too much about the danger that might lay around the corner. She told Viv about her moving to the newsroom and working with Steve. Viv was very happy for her. But still, they both kept checking on what was happening around them as they walked down the street. It would take a long time before that habit wore off.

CHAPTER 16

Next morning Emily had barely reached her new desk and said good morning to Steve when the phone rang. She answered it and was immediately on her guard because of the strange voice at the other end of the line. It was an unmistakeable fenland accent, but the man was speaking so quietly, that she could hardly hear him. She put her hand over her right ear to cut out the noise in the office, but that didn't help much.

'I'm sorry, but I can't hear what you are saying,' she said.

'Is that Emily Miller,' he said in a rasping voice.

'Yes,' she said, 'who are you?'

'Never mind who I am. Are you the woman who writes in the paper?' He sounded irritated.

'Yes, how can I help you?' she asked.

'It's how can I help you that matters. I know who murdered Harry Smithson.'

Emily instinctively grabbed her notebook and flicked it open. She said, in a deliberately loud voice. 'Did you say you know who murdered Harry Smithson?' Steve immediately looked up and carefully lifted the telephone extension.

'Yes, I know, and I am willing to tell you, but it's going cost you.'

'That could be arranged,' she said, looking at Steve for confirmation. He nodded.

'Never mind about 'could be arranged'. It has to be sorted before I tell you anything. Money up front and big money at that.'

'We can't just give you money up front without knowing how good your information is.'

'My information is straight from the horse's mouth. It's got to be money up front, and then I will tell you what I have.'

'I'm sorry, but we just couldn't agree to that. We would need to be very sure that you did know who carried out the murder,' she said, without bothering to look at Steve. 'Why don't we meet up and talk this through. If we believe that you really know who killed Smithson, we would be able to make arrangements for payment to be made.'

'It's got to be big money,' he said again. Softening his pitch a little.

'We can talk about that when we meet. You could come here to our offices, or we could come to meet you at home.'

'I'm not coming to your offices. That's a trip to Peterborough, and I'm not made of money.'

'OK, we will come to you. Where are you?'

'There's a café on the Guyhirn Straight. On your left about half a mile from Guyhirn.

'Yes, I know it,' she said, and Steve looked surprised.

'Be there at half past two this afternoon,' he said, 'and on your own.'

'Two-thirty is fine, but I won't be on my own. I couldn't take the decision to pay for your information, and I think you might be in a hurry to get your money. I'll bring someone who can make the decision.'

'Okay, that's better. I do need the money fast, so bringing someone who can make the decision is good. I'll be waiting in the far-right hand corner,' he said, in a voice full of hope and anticipation.

'By the way,' said Emily, 'you haven't told me your name.'

'No, and I'm not going to.'

'When we get to paying you, we will need to have a name,' she said.

'When you pay me, you can have it.' He rang off.

Steve managed to get a slightly larger car from the pool than Emily had for her trip to see Walter Green. This one, an Austin Cambridge, was a much smoother ride and did not bounce around as much as the Ford Anglia on the undulations of the Guyhirn straight.

'So,' said Steve as soon as they left the outskirts of the town behind them, 'do you come from a family of journalists?'

'No, my father is a solicitor in St Albans, and my mother is a…. well, a mother.'

'How did you end up in Peterborough?'

'Geoff Upthorne gave a lecture at my college and sold me on journalism. When this job came up, he put a word in for me.'

'Yes, he's somewhat of a legend at the paper. And from what I hear, he is a really good sort.'

'He has helped me a lot, with this case as well,' she said. 'He went through all his old notebooks and came up with Walter Green being a known associate of Harry Smithson.

'That's enough about me, what about you? Where is your hometown?'

'A little seaside resort called Cromer,' he said, 'You probably haven't heard of it.'

'Of course, I have,' she laughed. 'That was where we usually had our family holidays. I have spent many happy hours building sand castles and then watching the sea come in and wash them away. And going to the show at the end of the pier.'

'My father worked at a branch of a bank in Cromer, but he was killed in the war. My mother is still there. She turned the family home into a bed and breakfast. She had to to make ends meet, but to her surprise, it was quite successful, and it is still going strong. I got a job on the local rag in Norwich and worked my way up from there. Then I saw the an ad for a senior reporter in Peterborough and made the move.'

'Are you married?' Emily asked.

He turned and looked at her and then said, 'No 'I'm not.'

'A girlfriend?'

'There was one in Norwich, but she wouldn't move. We tried to keep the relationship going, but it soon became obvious to both of us that it wasn't going to work. Which I guess meant that it wasn't much of a relationship.'

'What about you?'

Emily hesitated. 'Well, there is a boy that I go out with from time to time, but I wouldn't call him a boyfriend.' She heard the words coming out of her mouth, but she couldn't believe that she had just said them. She had been feeling much closer to Terry recently and thought that this might be the real thing. But Steve was so open and relaxed with her, that she felt almost free to tell him anything. It was almost like she had known him for years.

He looked at her again but didn't say anything.

In no time at all, they saw the café on the left where they were to meet the mystery man who needed money quickly.

When Emily walked into the café, all eyes turned to look at her. Steve walked in behind her, and most people turned away again and pretended they weren't ogling her. It's funny how a girl on her own attracts so much more attention than when there is a man with her.

The smell of fried food was overpowering, and the sound of Elvis coming from the jukebox made it seem like a scene from a B-movie. Most of the people sitting at the tables looked like lorry drivers, but she had noticed a couple of cars and a tractor in the car park. They got two coffees at the counter and looked towards the far right of the room.

There was a lone man sitting near the window. They walked towards him, and Emily noticed that he seemed to be wearing an old RAF coat, several sizes too large for him, with the collar turned up. He was hunched forward so that only part of his face could be seen. Emily looked at his legs underneath the table and saw that he was wearing bicycle clips. Probably not a master criminal then, she thought.

Emily sat down at the table immediately in front of the man. Steve sat next to her.

'Hello, I'm Emily Miller, and this is Steve Moon.' She held her hand out, but he was not going to shake it.

'You're late,' he grumbled.

Emily looked at the clock on the wall. 'Two minutes early by that clock,' she said. The man ignored her.

'What is your name?'

'I'm not telling you that.'

She leant forwards and spoke slowly and clearly. 'Look, we have travelled out here at your request, because you have something you want us to buy. If you don't tell us your name and start acting like a grown man we are getting up and leaving. And you can try your luck with someone else.'

He looked at Steve, but he just smiled and shrugged his shoulders.

'What is your name?' she asked sharply.

'Sid,'

'Sid who?' she snapped back.

'Sid Slack.'

'That's better.' Emily said with a smile.

'Now, what have you got to tell us?'

'I know who it was that murdered Harry Smithson.'

'How do you know?'

'I overheard two men talking in a pub?' he said, taking a drink from the large mug of tea he was holding with both hands.

'Who were these two men? Steve asked.

Sid looked surprised that Steve had spoken but then shook his head. 'I can't tell you that,' he said.

'Do you know the names of the two men?' Emily asked.

'Of course, I know.'

'Who were they talking about?' Steve asked the question this time.

'The man who planned and carried out the murder.'

'Harry Smithson's murder?' Emily asked.

'No, another murder.'

Emily shook her head. 'So, you don't know who killed Harry Smithson. When you rang this morning, you said you knew who murdered the man that I had written about in the paper,' Emily said.

'I didn't mean that murder I meant another murder that no one knows about. I know who was murdered first, and I can guess who murdered Harry Smithson.'

'And you expect us to pay you to tell us about a murder that nobody seems to know has taken place and then believe your guess that you know who murdered Smithson is correct.' Steve joined in.

'You pay me, and I'll tell you straight away,' he said looking gloomily into his tea mug.

'Give us one name, just one of any of these people you are talking about.' Steve said.

'I can't do that. I need the money now. I owe a lot of money. Five hundred quid would do to start with, and I would trust you for the rest.'

Steve and Emily got up from the table.

'I gave you first chance, but now I'll go elsewhere. I've got someone lined up. You see.' He was still muttering to himself as Steve and Emily left the café.

'Do you think he knows anything?' Emily asked Steve as they got in the car.

'Maybe he does, or maybe he doesn't, but he can't expect us to hand him a wedge of money just on his word. We need a bit of proof. Five-hundred pounds - what planet is he living on?'

'And what was that about another murder? Do you think we might be dealing with two killings?' she asked.

'There seems to be some substance in what he is saying, but I think he is so concerned with his debt problems that he has lost all sense of reality. I think we have to try and make some more progress without him and only go back if we really have to. When you are obviously that strapped for cash, I guess you would make up any sort of story to try and make a bob or two.'

Steve and Emily were silent as they drove along the roads leading to Peterborough. Emily was turning over in her mind whether they were right in turning Sid Slack down. It may have been a chance to solve these mysteries quickly, but she also understood that they could not get the paper to agree to buy the information from such an unreliable source.

They were just a few hundred yards from the office when Emily said, 'What about Walter Green? He said he would let me know when he could tell me the truth. It's been several days, and I am getting concerned that he might keel over at any time. Then we would never know. Let's go and see him tomorrow.'

Next morning Emily had already arrived at her desk when Steve came in. They decided that they should go to see Walter Green as a matter of urgency before anything happened to him.

'We are just going to interview someone, but I should think we'll be out until lunchtime because it's near Wisbech' Steve said to the reporter sitting on the other side of him.

'A likely story,' someone shouted from the back of the room.

'That's what they call it now,' came from someone else.

Emily felt herself beginning to blush and hurried towards the door.

'You had all last night for that,' was the final call.

'Sorry about that,' said Steve, when they got outside. It's like being back at infant school, but everyone has to go through it at some time or other. They'll get over it.'

Emily laughed, 'I don't mind. It's good to be in a lively office, and I'll get them back sometime.'

The drive to Guyhirn seemed to take forever. There had been an accident, and the lorry involved had spilt a load of sugar beet all over the road. Eventually, they got past that, only to be stuck behind a long line of slow moving traffic following a tractor with a very large plough mounted on the back. This made overtaking almost impossible, as the tractor bounced alarmingly from side to side on the bumpy road surface. And if that wasn't enough they caught up with the bus to King's Lynn just after Thorney Toll and had to follow it all the way to their turn-off. It seemed to be driven by the most cautious and slowest driver in the world.

They arrived at the driveway and turned in only to be faced with a little old lady walking down the rough track towards them. They stopped, and Emily wound her window down.

'Oh, it's you,' she said, smiling with relief.

'You must be Elsie, where are you going? Can we give you a lift?' Emily asked.

'I'm just going down to the shop in the village' She pointed somewhere towards the east. Neither Steve or Emily could see any sign of a village.

'How far is it?' said Emily.

'It's only a couple of miles or so. I go down there twice a week.' She was a short, stocky woman, who looked full of determination and independence.

'Look, when we have finished having a chat with Walter, we can give you a lift to the village.'

She laughed heartily at the suggestion. 'It's very kind of you, but I don't need a lift, you'll have me getting soft.'

She started to walk away and then stopped. 'I'm glad you've come to see Walter. He's been very down lately, but after you had come to see him, he seemed to buck-up a little. But then he had this man come to see him. Late yesterday afternoon it was. On his bike. I don't know his name, but he's been around here for years. Anyway, he seems to have really shaken poor old Walter. He looks really bad again. So, you go and cheer him up.' And with that she set off at a steady pace, leaning determinedly forward into the brisk wind.

Steve parked the car in front of Walter's cottage. 'I think we can guess who the visitor was.'

'Yes, that's what I thought, and I noticed his bicycle clips in the café. It's not very far from the café to here, particularly if you are used to riding around in these sorts of conditions.' Emily said.

'People have told me stories of having to walk ten miles to school and back, even in snowy winters,' Steve said.

'Yes, they're hardy people in the fens. No doubt about it. It makes you feel pampered, doesn't it?' said Emily.

Walter met them at the door but was breathing very heavily from the effort of getting from his chair to the door. For a moment, he couldn't speak and just stood there holding on to the door.

'I'm glad you have come,' he gasped, leading them slowly through into his living room. It was much tidier today, and Emily guessed that Elsie had sorted it out before she went to the shop. Emily and Steve sat on the sofa, facing Walter. The springs on the sofa had gone, and Steve and Emily seemed to be almost sitting on the floor. They were looking up at Walter, who had added several cushions to his armchair, no doubt to make up for its lack of springs.

'We saw Elsie on the way in, and she said you have had a bit of an upset?' Emily said.

Walter hardly seemed to have noticed Steve. He kept his eyes on Emily all the time.

'Yes, that sneaky little rat Sid Slack came to blackmail me,' he said. Emily noticed a tear run down from his watery eye, which he quickly brushed away. 'Said he had heard me and Harry talking in the pub. Bloody nosey little sod. And after all these years.'

'What were you and Harry talking about in the pub?' she asked.

'It's like I told you before. Things we shouldn't have been saying in public,' he replied. 'It was me really. Not Harry. Harry didn't want to hear what I was saying. Kept telling me to shut up. But you know what it's like when the drink takes hold.'

Emily didn't really because, on the occasions that she had drunk too much, with the hockey crowd mainly, she had fallen asleep. Several times the other girls used to have to wake her up to go home.

'What were you talking about that was so important?' She tried again.

Walter ignored the question. 'He said he would sell the story to the papers if I didn't give him the money.

'Do you believe him?' she asked. 'Do you really think he heard anything?'

Walter shook his head. 'I just don't know. He may be bluffing, but I can't afford to take a chance. I wouldn't put it passed the cheeky little bugger to go to the police and see if he could get some money out of them.'

'But does it matter Walter,' she said. 'You said that you are going to tell us soon, so why not now, and then he can't blackmail you.'

'He's already had nearly fifty quid out of the biscuit tin. That's all I'd got. Now Elsie has to buy my groceries.'

'If you tell us now, all this will go away,' Emily said. 'Tell us about what you did and who you were working with, and Sid Slack has nothing to blackmail you with.'

'You don't understand,' he wheezed. 'This has got to be done properly. The timing is important to me because I am not ready to give in yet.' He pointed at his chest. 'It's going to win I know, but I still want as much time as I can.' As if to remind himself of his own mortality, he started to cough, quietly at first, but rising to a crescendo. He lay back gasping for air.

Emily stood up, because she felt she needed to do something, but didn't know what. Her knowledge of medical matters was zero. 'I'll get you a glass of water,' she said, happy that at least she had thought of something.

'No, no, no,' Walter gasped. 'It's gone now I'm okay.'

'But you're not okay, are you Walter? And the game you are playing is a very dangerous one.'

'What Emily is telling you is true Walter. Listen to her please,' Steve spoke for the first time, and Walter looked slightly surprised as if he had forgotten that Steve was there.

'She is being put in great danger because of this. Billy Pope and his thug stepbrothers have chased and nearly caught her in the dark of the Cathedral precincts. And Arnold Lackford has tried to get her fired from the paper. You know she's a nice person, and I'm sure you wouldn't want anything to happen to her.'

Walter looked across at Emily, and she thought he was going to cry again. 'No, I wouldn't want anything to happen to a lovely little old gal like her. I'll call my friend and tell him that Sid Slack is coming to see him and that he is trying to blackmail us both. He will pay him off, he's never short of money.

'I was going to tell him about me wanting to clear my conscience before I'm called. Give him a chance to get away and start again somewhere else. But deep down I knew that wouldn't be possible. He will have to answer for what he did. Like we both should have done. And maybe, me getting TB, was how I've had to pay the price.'

'Are you religious Walter?' Emily asked, feeling a bit uncomfortable about the things he was saying. 'We can ask the local vicar to call round if that would help.'

Walter thought about it for a minute and then said, 'No, I can't say I'm religious, and the vicar gives me the creeps, so I'll do this myself. By the end of this week, I will get it sorted, and you can come back, and I will tell you everything.'

'How are you going to get in touch with your friend?' Emily asked.

'Elsie has a phone that she lets me use.'

'Ah, that's good,' she said, having thought that he might have to walk to a phone box in the village.

They stood up to leave, and as Steve walked past Walter, he handed him several pound notes. 'That's from the newspaper to thank you for your help. You'll be able to pay for your groceries now.'

'Thank you,' Walter brightened up a little. 'That's very good of you. I hate taking money from Elsie after all she does for me.'

'That was a very nice gesture,' Emily said as they drove down towards the road.

'It was the least I could do really because when we refused to pay for Sid Slack's rambling nonsense, he came straight here and put the screws on poor old Walter. I'll put it on expenses. They make allowances for random payments when it's necessary to get some information for a story.'

147

'This is all so surreal,' Emily said, shaking her head. 'Geoff said as a trainee journalist I would be working on cosy little stories about garden fetes, church hall events, bring and buy stalls and the odd shoplifting incident.

'Instead, I am dealing with one, two or possibly three murders, tracing returning soldiers from fourteen years ago and being chased around the Cathedral by a knife wielding idiot.'

'Yes, the way it has worked out you have had a rough ride. It must have been very frightening at times. You must have wondered what sort of a job you had let yourself in for. It all comes back to John Cadham not taking the story seriously. You have done a damn good job without any help from him. I think you are going to go far in this profession.'

Emily looked at Steve as he drove. 'What are you looking at?' he said.

'I was just waiting for the punchline,' she said. 'I never know when you are serious or just kidding around.'

'What I just said is real. If we can get through this without anybody else getting killed or hurt, we are going to have one hell of a good story. And you are going to get full credit for what you have achieved.'

'If we can get through alive?' she said with a smile.

'Yes, I would say that is the minimum requirement.'

'Do you think we can afford to wait until Friday before we can go back to see Walter?' he said.

'I think we have to, he is a stubborn old bugger, and it took a lot for him to agree to a firm date. If you hadn't played the do you want to be responsible for Emily getting killed card, I don't think he would have agreed.

'I think tomorrow I will ring Geoff and tell him where we have got to and ask him to give us any other names that have any links to Smithson, Green, Lackford or Pope. I know it's a long shot, but it could throw something up. And at least it seems that we are doing something while we wait to go back to see Walter.'

She called Geoff Upthorne the next day and filled him in with the latest developments. He was relieved to hear that Steve was fully behind the story and promised that he would look through his notebook later that morning and get back to her.

Emily decided to go without lunch because she felt sure that Geoff would call back as quickly as he could. It was fifteen minutes past one when her extension rang.

Geoff got straight down to business. He said that he had found just three names that probably had links to Green, but there must be many more because

Green had spent all his life doing odd jobs for people. He said many people had to work like that, because of the nature of the agriculture in this part of England. It was mainly fruit and vegetable picking and, therefore, very seasonal. Green was a little luckier than most because he also had a smallholding of about half an acre adjoining his cottage.

'So,' said Geoff, 'I'll give you the three names I have, but it will be just a shot in the dark. I've nothing to suggest that they have done anything wrong.'

'Yes, that's all I was expecting. This is almost just passing the time until I can get back to see Green again on Friday, but I can't just sit here doing nothing.'

Geoff read out to her the list of people. 'There was Charlie Dobson, a gangmaster from Friday Bridge.'

Emily asked, 'What is a gangmaster?' Thinking he must be some sort of criminal warlord.

Geoff explained that he got gangs of fruit and vegetable pickers together to undertake work for the farmers and fruit growers.

'Green used to do a lot of work for him, in fact, Dobson was probably his main source of income. But he won't be easy to find because I understand that he retired a few years ago and went to live somewhere in Lancashire, to be near his daughter. I don't think he is a strong contender because there is nothing to show that Dobson was anything other than a hardnosed businessman. Gangmasters are seldom the most popular people around because of the nature of their work. Farmers think they are ripping them off and the pickers think that they are taking too big a cut from their wages.

'I probably won't put him on the top of my list, but I will if the other two fail,' Emily said.

'The next name is Ron Tilbrooke, a fruit and veg wholesaler, who has a house and warehouse somewhere between March and Chatteris. You will get his full address from the telephone directory. There is no reason to believe that he is involved with anything dodgy. He's got a successful business. It seems that he and Green went to school together and were both a bit wild and got into a few scrapes. But nothing violent as far as I can see. Nicking cars to go joyriding seemed to be their main activity, but since they grew up neither, he or Tilbrooke seemed to have stepped out of line.'

'Is March far from here?' She asked.

'No, can't be more than twenty miles.'

'We will pay him a visit then.'

'This one is probably more promising. Barry Farrow. He has a smallholding next to Green's plot. They had a big falling out because Green accused him of moving the boundary between their land and pinching some of his. But this doesn't mean they might have been partners in any crime.'

'Unless Farrow thought he could get away with pinching some of his land because he knew what

Green had done. Maybe Green was the one who planned and carried out the crime,' Emily said.

'Yes, that is another possibility. You just have to keep an open mind and go digging.'

CHAPTER 17

She put the phone down after speaking to Geoff and turned to tell Steve about the latest developments, but he was not there. That was most unusual. Steve was never first in and seldom looked if he was fully awake when he did arrive, but he was never last.

She was becoming a little concerned when he came striding along the corridor. He dropped into his chair and smiled at Emily.

'I was beginning to wonder where you were,' she said.

Steve leant forward and spoke quietly to Emily. 'I got in early so that I could bring Martin Yates up to speed with the story. It occurred to me that we may be fully occupied with this over the next week or so, and wanted to be sure that he is okay with that. He agrees that this could be big and is going to let us concentrate solely on it until it's done. But, he would like it to be sooner rather than later.

'Wouldn't we all,' Emily said.

'What he will be worried about is word getting around about the story and the Nationals getting a sniff of it. We need to keep everything to ourselves from now on. A lot of local journalists augment their income by acting as stringers for the nationals. There is no real harm in that if they play fair with their main employers, the locals. If they let them go to press first and then feed it to the nationals that is fine.

'Some people in this room know what we are doing, but they don't know how far we are from going to press. So, everything must remain between you and me from now on. And that includes Viv, Pete and even the police. Geoff's okay because he will understand completely and it won't go further than him.'

Emily nodded and then said, 'I am glad to hear that because I had a long chat with Geoff while you were in with Martin. We had better go somewhere that we can talk in private and decide our next move.'

'That's been taken care of. Collect your stuff, and I will show you,' he said.

They collected their paperwork together, stuffed it all into a battered old briefcase that Steve produced from under his desk and walked out of the office ignoring the shouts of 'nice of you to drop in' and 'have a good weekend'.

Steve said that although they would come to the office as often as they could, it would be just to collect messages. They were going to base themselves at a small office just off Queen Street. It was basically a large garage, with a huge door that couldn't have seen any paint since before the war. Next to that was an ordinary sized front door, which led up a flight of stairs to a surprisingly tidy, but slightly dusty, office. The garage and the room behind the office seemed to be full of back copies of newspapers and magazines as well as rollers and other used parts from printing presses.

In the office, there were two very big, but well-worn desks. The polished deep brown wood was inlaid with faded red leather covering the main surface. They looked as though they had once been very grand. Two, equally worn leather chairs stood behind the desks. Both had a fine view of a brick wall across the street.

Emily found a duster and quickly removed the thin film of dust on the desks and chairs. They opened the briefcase, emptied the contents onto the desks and sorted it into small piles. She then took her notebook out and ran through the list that Geoff Upthorne had given her.

'What do you suggest?' Steve said.

'To start with let's put Charlie Dobson to one side. He doesn't seem to have much contact with Green, and he's going to take several days to track down and interview,' she said.

'Agreed,' said Steve.

'Ron Tilbrooke, seems to be a bit of a long shot to me. They were friends when they were kids, but nothing they did was really bad, and they seemed to have drifted apart when they grew up,' she said.

'Worth a visit, just to check him out, would you say?' Steve asked.

'Absolutely, it's not far to his warehouse and face to face is a lot better than a telephone call.'

'What about Barry Farrow?'

'I think he is a lot more interesting. I'd like to hear both sides of the boundary dispute, but we don't even know how long ago it was. Once again, face to face will help,' she said.

'I don't know about you, but I still think Billy Pope or Arnold Lackford are more likely candidates,' Steve said. 'They both reacted over aggressively to your stories. Not the actions of men with nothing to hide.'

Emily laughed. 'We'd better wait until we have spoken to these two. You never know, we might be in for a lively day.'

To their surprise the very old telephone on the desk was still connected, so Emily called Tilbrooke and without any questions being asked, she was put through.

'Hello, Tilbrooke Fruit and Veg?'

'Is that Mr Tilbrooke?' she asked.

'Yes, speaking.'

'My name is Emily Miller, and I work for the local newspaper in Peterborough. We have been covering a story about the murder of Harry Smithson, fourteen years ago. You may have seen it.'

'Yes, I have, as a matter of fact. Very strange business. But I don't see how I can help in any way. I never met the man.'

'It's really the people he might have known that we are trying to track down, but after all these years it is difficult. We have a list of names, and you might be able to help us find some of them. We won't take up much of your time.'

'I don't think I can help, but you a very welcome to come over. Any time today will be okay for me. I'll be in the warehouse.'

Emily put the phone down and looked across at Steve. 'Well, he sounded a decent sort. No problems talking to us and we can go over now. I don't know whether to be disappointed or pleased.'

'Let's reserve judgement until we see him. I don't really go along with the popular thinking that you can see a murderer by the look in his eyes. I think history shows that meek and friendly men and women can be just as capable of killing as any wild-eyed bully.'

'Well his telephone manner was excellent, so let's get over there and find out for ourselves,' she said with a laugh.

'Ok, I'll give Betty a ring and tell her where we are going, so she can let Martin know that we are on the case. Now he has given us his full support; we need to keep him in the picture as much as possible.' Steve said.

They got the address out of the two-year-old telephone directory and studied the map that Steve had brought with him.

'One other thing before we go,' Emily said. 'I know we can't share any new information we have with Mike Townsend, but I do think it would be wise just to keep in touch. We might need some help from him. When this is solved, we will have to pass over all the evidence, and for long term relationships it would be good to know we are both on the same side.'

'What did you have in mind?' he asked.

'I could ask him if he could check on the names Ron Tilbrooke and Barry Farrow, just to see if they have any sort of criminal records. I'll tell him that they are just names that Geoff had turned up from his old notebooks, so they probably won't lead us anywhere, but anything is worth a try at this stage.'

Steve thought it over for a few moments and then said, 'Yes, that's a good idea. He hasn't heard from you for a while, so might be wondering if you had cut him out. And at the same time, we get to know if they have any previous convictions for anything.'

Emily made the call and checked whether it was alright for Mike to talk at that moment. He said it was and took a note of the two names.

'They don't ring any bells for me, but I will get them checked out. I take it that things are not moving along very quickly.'

'Yes, it is a bit like that at the minute. One minute you think you're getting somewhere and the next you're back where you started,' Emily said.

'That's the story of my life,' Mike laughed. 'Call me tomorrow morning, and I will tell you anything we have.'

CHAPTER 18

Neither Emily or Steve were great when it came to maps, and the map that Steve had found at the office was such a small scale that many place names were not shown. They made their way through Whittlesey and Coates. Then they passed through a little collection of cottages. After that, they seemed to be caught in a kind of maze that consisted of one railway crossing after another, and then another. What's more, all the gates seemed to be closed to road traffic and were opened by disgruntled looking railwaymen who looked as though cars were just a necessary evil.

'I'm sure we have come the wrong way, there must be a better road than this.' Emily said.

'Yes, I'm sure there is, but we're not going back through those again. You could see how grumpy they looked when they came to open the crossing gates. You'd think the Flying Scotsman was due any minute.'

'They call it the Three Horseshoes, which is very appropriate.' Emily said. 'I have just found it on the map.'

It was almost October, and the signs of Autumn were beginning to spread across the flat, desolate fenlands. They came to the small market town of March, turned right at the market place and headed out of town towards Chatteris. A couple of miles further on they turned left onto a narrow road with a line of Poplars down one side and a steep half-filled dyke on the other.

After about two hundred yards they could see a red and yellow painted sign for Tilbrooke Fruit and Veg Wholesalers. The sign was professionally produced and fixed to the side of the large brick building, which seemed to be comparatively new and as they came closer, they could see an identical sign was fixed to the front of the building. There were three large trucks parked next to the warehouse, with two others being loaded through the large front doors.

'So, this is the Tilbrooke empire,' said Steve. 'Looks like a substantial business. And look at the house next door.' It was also a new building with cream bricks and large bay windows. Roman columns and portico enhanced the front entrance.

'Wow!' said Emily. 'I wasn't expecting that. I bet the people living in the caravan next door are impressed.'

'By the way, 'Steve said. 'I think we should do this without notebooks. If he has something to hide, we don't want to spook him.'

Emily nodded. 'Good idea.'

As soon as Emily and Steve had stepped out of the car, a man came out of the warehouse and walked towards them.

'You managed to find us alright?' he said cheerfully. 'We are a bit out of the way here.'

'Yes, and I've never seen so many level crossings so close together,' Steve said.

'Oh, you came that way. You should have stuck to the main road.'

'We will, going back,' said Steve.

'Ron Tilbrooke,' he said, holding out a hand towards Emily. 'And you must be Emily'

They shook hands, and Emily introduced Steve. Ron Tilbrooke was in his mid-fifties, Emily guessed. He had the lined, weather-beaten face of a man who lived most of his life outside. His eyes were narrow, probably through squinting into the sunlight. He had the slightly reserved manner of an introvert, who found small talk difficult. He was also quite softly spoken so that he could hardly be heard above the machinery that was loading crates of produce into one of the trucks.

He led them in through the large warehouse doors, to a small office in the corner.

'We can talk in my office,' he said. As soon as Emily and Steve sat down in the two chairs he had placed in front of his desk; he began to make coffee from a kettle and jar of Nescafe, which were standing on the top of a filing cabinet.

'I didn't ask, but would you like a coffee?' he said.

Steve said he would, and although Emily didn't really want one, she said yes because she had seen him put the coffee into three cups. They both said yes to milk and sugar, and Tilbrooke carefully placed the cups in front of them.

He was dressed like a gentleman farmer, with a green wax jacket, matching Wellington boots and black corduroy trousers, tucked into his boots. The outfit was topped off with a tweed flat cap, from which his plentiful grey hair sprang out in all directions.

'So,' he said, as he sat down behind his desk, how can I help?'

'You probably can't,' said Emily, 'this is just a long shot. Steve and I have been trying to piece together what might have happened to Harry Smithson, who seems to have been murdered on his return to Peterborough, just after the war. After fourteen years people forget, so it is proving a very slow job for us.

'What we are doing at the moment is trying to find people who might have known anyone who had a grudge against Smithson. We've had a few suggestions and a few names given to us. One of these is Walter Green, who we know was quite a close friend of Smithson. Your name came up simply because we understand that you and Walter were friends from schooldays.'

'Yes, that is going back a few years,' said Tilbrooke. 'I have to admit we were a bit wild in those days. I guess our names came up because we had one or two skirmishes with the law at that time. But when you start to get a bit older and wiser, plus getting some family commitments, that sort of nonsense goes out the window.'

'Do you still see Walter?' Steve asked.

Tilbrooke shook his head. 'No, not for many years now. I did help him out with one or two money troubles he had, but that was five or six years ago. We just grew apart. I was ambitious and wanted to get on, Walter was just happy as he was.'

'Did he work for you?' Emily asked.

'Yes, I gave him a job soon after starting this business. But that was a very long time ago, before the war in fact. There was only two or three of us in those days. We started selling fruit and veg door to door. It was a stupid idea for a business in these parts. People around here grow their own, or trade with their neighbours, for fruit and veg.

'It's in the big towns where there is real money to be made, so we started buying it here and trucking it directly into the towns and selling to shops. It's mainly Birmingham and Manchester that we serve. Walter didn't want to drive a truck, and that was all I could offer him at the time, so he left and made a living doing odd jobs and fruit picking in the season.

'I didn't hear much from him after that. He got into debt a couple of times, but it was never much he wanted, and I was happy to help him out for old time's sake. A nice chap is Walter, but he's not a go-getter. Just wants a quiet life and there's nothing wrong with that.'

'I saw him a few days ago, and he's not well,' said Emily. It's TB, and I honestly don't think he's got long.'

'I'm sorry to hear that,' Tilbrooke said. 'I'll have to find the time to go over and see him. Typical Walter, not to let me know. He would would think that I would be too busy to help him. Did he mention me to you?'

'No, I didn't have your name then, and he never said anything,' she replied.

'No, I don't suppose he would. The way Walter lived, just scratching a living here and there, means you are constantly meeting new people. They come and go with the seasons.'

'As an old friend, I think he would welcome a visit from you,' Emily said.

'I can't get away for the next few days. We are really busy at the moment, and you can't afford to let customers down in this business. But I will try and get to see him next week.'

'I am sorry, we have taken up too much of your time already.' Emily said.

'No problem at all and it gave me the chance to get a coffee break.'

As they drove away from the warehouse, Emily said, 'What do you think of him?'

'He seemed okay to me. He's either a very accomplished actor, or he genuinely has nothing to hide,' Steve said. 'I know there are people who can just turn the charm on and off at will, but somehow he didn't seem the sort. I quite liked him. So that just leaves us with Billy Pope, Lackford or Barry Farrow.'

'Or,' added Emily, 'Green himself, who after two visits has not really told us anything worth knowing.'

CHAPTER 19

By the time Steve and Emily had returned to the office, Viv had gone home, so Emily decided to walk on her own. She had only taken a few steps down the street, when a passing Lambretta scooter, braked suddenly and then swerved towards her on the pavement. Emily stepped back in surprise, before recognising Steve sitting on what looked like a brand-new machine. It was turquoise and white, and Emily loved it at first sight.

'Sorry if I startled you,' he said with a grin. 'Were you going to walk home on your own?'

'Yes, Viv has gone.'

'And what did I say about being safe?'

She shrugged her shoulders. 'I thought I would be okay; Billy Pope seems to be lying low.'

'Come on, jump on.'

'I thought you said I should be keeping safe?'

'This is safe. I promise.'

Emily was very pleased she was wearing her drainpipes. New ones, in fact, bought only last Saturday with some sporty pumps. Being small and agile, she balanced herself on Steve's arm and then in one quick movement was sitting on the pillion seat, leaning comfortably against the padded backrest.

'No crash helmets?' she said over his shoulder.

'I've got some at home?'

'That's good to know,' she laughed.

And they were off. The traffic was thinning now the rush hour was over, and Steve expertly weaved his way along Cowgate, over Crescent Bridge and along Thorpe Road.

As they got near to Emily's flat, Steve turned and said, 'Do you fancy going for a drink?'

Without waiting for a second, she replied, 'Yes, that would be great.'

They continued along Thorpe Road to Longthorpe and Steve turned into the small car park of the Fox and Hounds. It was busy inside, mainly populated with men dropping in for a pint on the way home. Heads turned when they walked in, with most eyes fixed on Emily.

She smiled and said hello and the drinkers turned back to their conversations. Steve bought the drinks, and they walked to a table in the corner. Emily was still feeling the exhilaration of the scooter ride, but there was something else that she sensed was giving her an excited light-headedness. She thought for a moment about what it could be. She had hardly eaten anything since this morning. It could be that. She had put the pressure and worry about the Smithson killing to the back of her mind so that it couldn't be that.

She looked across at Steve, and it suddenly became clear. It was being with Steve. It was being close and holding him when they were on the Scooter. It was knowing that he would look after her.

She suddenly realised that she hadn't had much of a life since she came to Peterborough. Viv is a wonderful friend and had helped her so much, but that is what she was, just a friend. When you leave home, you are glad to be free to do what you want and go your own way. But that doesn't replace the unconditional love that you get from your parents. That can only be replaced when the right person comes along, and Emily was beginning to feel that way about Steve. She wished she could tell him and ask him if he felt the same way about her.

'You're very quiet,' Steve said, 'didn't you enjoy the ride on the scooter?'

She smiled, 'Yes, it was great, and I'm really enjoying myself. You've been good to me at work, and now, you've made me happy again tonight.'

He leant forward and squeezed her hand. 'You are a remarkable girl Emily, and I hope that we can have lots of nice nights like this.'

She almost felt she was going to cry for a moment, but that would never do. 'I would like that very much,' she said, looking intently into his eyes to see if she could tell how he felt about her.

'What about Terry?' he said as if sensing what she had been thinking.

'It was never really right with Terry,' she said. 'He's nice, but not a lot of fun. Life is very serious for Terry, and I like to have fun. He never was a proper boyfriend. I always thought of him as just a friend. I will find a way to tell him.'

'In the meantime, to all those clowns in the office, we are just working on this story together, we are just work colleagues,' he said.

'Yes, we don't want to prove them right as quickly as that,' she laughed.

They finished their drinks and then drove down to the nearest fish and chip shop and ate them sitting on the wall outside. 'I know how to treat a girl on a first date,' he said.

He dropped Emily off at her flat, and she ran up the stairs. Viv was sitting in the living room watching TV.

'You're late tonight, have you been working?' Viv asked.

'No, I went for a drink with Steve and then we got some fish and chips.'

'So, tell me more,' said Viv.

'There is nothing more. He gave me a lift on his scooter and then asked if I wanted a drink.'

'So, what are you thinking? Could it turn into something more serious?' Viv persisted.

'I think that sometime soon we will get together, but not just now,' Emily said.

'At the moment, we have the Smithson murder story to sort out, and Martin Yates has told us to work away from the office to reduce the possibility of leaks.'

'Leaks, to where?'

'You know how the Nationals have a habit of pinching scoops from under the noses of the locals, well that's where the need for secrecy comes in. So, I am not allowed to tell anyone about where we are going, or any details of the story. After what happened to John Cadham it is a safety issue as well.'

Viv looks at little bit taken aback, but she nodded that she understood.

'And, incidentally, that goes for our private lives too,' Emily added.

'You can trust me,' Viv said with a laugh.

'I know I can because I'm not going to tell you anything.'

'But you do feel just a bit excited about you and Steve, don't you?' Viv asked.

'I'm in shock still. It just hit me out of the blue. Suddenly it was all so obvious that that was what I wanted.'

'And what did he say?'

'I can't remember really. It's just a mist, a jumble of words. But he looked as happy as me.'

CHAPTER 20

The next morning, Emily arrived at her desk, and Steve was already there. They greeted each other, as usual, with a cheery 'good morning'. She sat down at her desk and started sifting through the few items of post that had arrived overnight. There was nothing of any importance, and she guessed that most had been filtered out for others to deal with.

She desperately wanted to look at Steve, just to reassure herself that he hadn't changed his mind overnight. It was stupid, she knew that, but she still wanted to look at him. When she did, he was looking down at something he was reading. It then occurred to her that he was probably avoiding looking at her for the same reason.

'How are you this morning?' she asked.

He looked up and grinned. 'I couldn't be better,' he replied. 'What about you?'

'Same with me,' she said. They looked into each other's eyes, a little longer than they might have done the day before and then turned away. Emily realised that it would not be easy during these days of pretending that there was nothing happening between them. She could always tell when her friends crossed over from friendship to love. So why did they think that people wouldn't know? I guess we all think we can disguise it, but in reality, we can't.

'I think we ought to be going,' she said, thinking the less time we are here, the less chance I have of giving our secret away. The real problem is that she was so happy about it, she wanted to tell everyone.

'Yes okay,' he replied, in a matter of fact way. Maybe he was good at hiding his feelings.

They left the office and walked to their temporary base in the storeroom office. Steve opened the door, and they walked up the stairs. As soon as they got into the dusty old office, she turned to him, and he pulled her close, and they kissed. He held her tightly to him, and he said, 'I wanted to do this last night...'

'...but the fish and chips came between us,' she finished his sentence off, and they both laughed. They were both happy now, it was real, and they were ready to get on with their work.

Firstly, she called Mike Townsend to find out if he had discovered anything from the past on Tilbrooke and Farrow. The answer was nothing at all on Farrow, but plenty on Tilbrooke and Green. There was a two-year period, 1935 to early 1937, when they had a dozen, mainly minor offences, such as taking a car without the owner's consent, driving under age and without a license, causing damage to cars, and some theft prosecutions. Most of them car related.

Mike said that this sort of thing was not unusual for boys in the fens, particularly because the

1930s had brought so much poverty everywhere. Finding a job was extremely difficult, and family life inevitably suffered. There was very little for young people to do and they were rebelling against a society that seemed to have abandoned them. Making a nuisance of themselves, not only made them feel that they were somebody, but it also brightened their otherwise very dull lives.

'I'm not excusing their behaviour, but I have often thought that if I was a kid growing up in those circumstances, I might easily have been tempted. Particularly, if I was the odd one out,' Mike said. 'So, don't put too much importance on their records, it was happening to a lot of young lads in those days, and on a much smaller scale, it still is now.'

Emily thanked him for the information and the insight into life in the 1930s.

They started by trying to find an address for Barry Farrow. There was nothing in the telephone directory, which wasn't surprising because many people did not have a telephone. They decided that they might as well go to the village nearest to Walter's house because the smallholding couldn't be far away.

They drove past Walter's house and turned left at the next junction. After another half mile, they came to the village that Elsie walked to twice a week.

'Two and a half miles each way, ten miles a week and five of those carrying groceries. Life certainly can be tough in the fens,' said Steve. 'And how old would you say Elsie is?'

'It's difficult to say, she looks over sixty, but with a tough life like that, she's probably only mid-fifties,' Emily replied.

He stopped the car outside the general stores, which also doubled as the post office. There was a butcher's shop next door and a pub across the road. Emily also noted that there was a bus stop, that must run to Wisbech or Peterborough, or maybe both.

There were no customers in the shop, but the shop owner was whistling happily to himself as he tipped mud covered potatoes into a box at the front of the fruit and vegetable counter.

He looked up as Emily and Steve came into the shop and called, 'I'll be with you in a minute.'

Steve walked towards him and said, 'No, please don't stop what you are doing, we only want to ask you a question.'

'Well, ask away,' he said putting the sack of potatoes in the back room.

'We are looking for Barry Farrow?' Steve said.

'What's he been up to this time?' Steve detected a slight Northern Irish accent.

'It's nothing really. We are with the local paper and have been running a story about a smallholding boundary dispute. We just need to get Mr Farrow's side of the story.' Steve said.

'Well good luck to you if you are looking for the truth,' said the shopkeeper.

'Why do you say that?' Emily joined the discussion.

'Because the truth and Barry Farrow are seldom seen in the same room,' the shopkeeper said with a laugh.

'You're not from around these parts, are you? Northern Ireland, is it?' Steve asked.

'You've got it in one,' he said with a chuckle. 'The other day one of the people in the village asked me if I was Polish, but I did find out later that she was stone deaf. I can tell that you've got an ear for accents. Everyone round here call me Mac because they can't pronounce my Irish name and I like the sound of Mac. Nice and simple, just like me.'

'I'm Emily, and this is Steve.' They shook hands with Mac.

'Why did you come here of all places,' Emily asked.

'It's the old troubles back home. I could see that it was slowly getting worse. Irishmen fighting Irishmen, I wanted no part of it, so here I am. I see myself as a missionary. I am trying to get the people of the village talking to each other. They hardly say anything to you. Just grunt and mumble at each other. They think I'm wasting their time by talking to them. But I say there is nothing better than good crack.'

'What's good crack?' Emily laughed.

'It's a good chat or gossip. It's what makes the world go round. But I went off the subject a bit there, you were asking me about Barry Farrow? In plain and simple terms, he's a lying little toe rag'

'He is no friend of yours then?' said Steve.

'He's no friend of anyone in the village. His house is full of stuff he's pinched, and he owes me three pounds, twelve shillings, and sixpence. I let him run up a bill, and when I ask him for the money, he said he had paid my wife when I wasn't here. I thought it was strange that she hadn't left a note for me. She would usually put one in the till. Of course, it was a complete lie, and I haven't seen him since. But let's look on the bright side. If that keeps him out of my shop, it's worth every penny of what he owes me.'

'So, where can we find him?' said Emily. 'He sounds like a lovely person,'

'You just came down the road from the A47. I saw you stop outside. Go back that way and when you pass the last house in the village, its only about five hundred yards down the road. There is a small track on your left that runs around to the back of the other houses. At the end of that is an old brick barn that Farrow has converted into a sort of house.

'And a piece of advice for you.' Mac continued. 'Don't drive all the way in and park at his front door, because he will be out through the back door and off in his truck before you can stop him. There is a little bridge over a dried-up dyke, about forty yards from his house. The track narrows where the bridge is, so park on that and walk. And don't worry, he won't try ramming your car because his truck wouldn't survive a collision with a bicycle, let alone a car.'

They thanked Mac for his advice, and the crack, and walked out to the car.

'Well, that was a pleasant surprise. A real character, but Barry sounds a slimy git. I think we are going to love him,' Steve said.

'Should we pretend to be debt collectors, after the money he owes Mac,' Emily said laughing.

'I've got news for you Emily; you look about as much like a debt collector as I look like a Parish priest.'

'I think you would look quite good with one of those little white collars and the long dress, red I think,' she said.

Steve just shook his head and started the car. They followed Mac's instructions and were soon driving down a muddy little track. It turned sharp left after a short distance and there, in front of them, they could see the house where Barry Farrow lived. It was quite small and looked as though it was about to collapse. But Emily thought it had probably looked like that for a hundred years.

It was strange because its dimensions seemed to be challenging any normal building techniques. It was small, but it was also surprisingly tall and looked almost as if it was top-heavy. It had probably once been a storage barn, with a loft. But most of it had either fallen down or been demolished. It had few windows, and those it did have were spread haphazardly throughout the tiny building. Nothing lined up with anything.

As they sat looking at the house, they suddenly noticed someone running across the field behind the house. It took them a second or two to realise what had happened.

'I think that might be Barry doing a runner,' Steve said.

The tall, stick-like figure, stumbled and staggered along the rutted soil that looked newly ploughed. 'Yes, and he looks quite keen to get away from us,' Emily said.

'That must come out on a road somewhere, let's see if we can drive round and catch him coming out the other side,' Steve suggested.

Emily grabbed the map and followed the road with her finger. 'It looks a long way, but I'm sure we can get there faster than he can run through a ploughed field.'

Steve started the car and swung it round sharply in the small area in front of the house. Emily noticed that the thin shape of Farrow was already difficult to pick out against the blackness of the soil. They drove quickly around the roads, taking two left turns, before joining a slightly bigger road that probably was the one that he was heading for. Steve slowed the car down, and Emily scanned the field for any sign of movement.

Then she saw him, quite close to the road ahead. Steve slowed further, and a car behind overtook them. Farrow was frantically clambering over a five-bar gate. He nearly staggered into the road but righted himself just as the car in front was approaching him. He waved his thumb frantically at the car, which swerved to miss him and then drove on. Steve slowed the car.

'What's he doing?' said Emily. 'He's thumbing a lift from us.'

Steve laughed. 'I think he was so keen to make a dash for it; he didn't even notice what sort of car we had or who was in it. Let's see.'

Steve braked and stopped, just a few yards past him.

He ran to the car and Emily wound her window down.

'Can we give you a lift?'

'Yes please,' Barry said eagerly.

'Jump in then, we are only going to the next village,' Steve said.

'That will do very nicely, thank you.'

'How far is the next village?' Steve asked.

'About five miles.'

'Good. That will give us time to explain who we are and why we wanted a chat with you. Firstly, we are not debt collectors. We are from the local newspaper and just wanted to get your side of the story in this boundary dispute you are having with Walter Green.'

'Bloody hell. Are you telling me I just ran like a fucking lunatic across those fields for nothing? Christ, I thought I was going to have a heart attack.'

'We didn't make you run,' said Steve. 'We just wanted to talk.'

'Yes, I've heard that one before as well.' said Farrow grumpily.

'It's true,' said Emily. We couldn't believe it when you ran off like that. We are just here to get your side of the story.'

'And another thing,' said Steve. 'If you answer our questions as truthfully as possible, without any bullshit, there's a tenner in it for you.'

Farrow was silent.

'What's the matter?' said Steve. 'Have you forgotten what a tenner looks like or do you want to know the meaning of truthful?'

'I want to know where the catch is?'

'There is no catch. Just answer some simple questions. We are not asking you to grass on anyone, although I don't think that would be any problem for you, would it Barry?'

He thought some more and then said 'OK, what do you want to know?'

'That's, better.' He slowed the car down and turned into a short track that led to a closed field gate.

Steve got out the car and got into the other rear passage seat. Farrow nervously watched him.

'What are you doing?' Farrow looked as if he expected Steve to attack him.

'Just want to see your eyes when you answer the questions. I have been trained to be able to spot a lie, instantly.'

'Emily has a few questions for you. I am going to decide if your answers are true.' He fixed his eyes on Farrow's face and said, 'Okay Emily, I'm watching him.'

She turned in her seat so that she could see Farrow's face as well. 'Why did you say that Walter Green had said that you could have the extra land,'

Farrow squirmed in his seat and then said, 'Well he never seems to use it anymore, so I thought that he wouldn't mind if I did.'

'But you didn't actually ask him?' Emily persisted.

After a short silence, Farrow said, 'No, but I was going to.'

'That's a lie,' Steve said, and you've only had two questions and answered one with a lie. Not good Barry. Next time the tenner goes down to a fiver.'

'I won't do it again,' mumbled Farrow.

'Are you going to press on with your claim that the boundary was incorrectly marked?'

'No, no. I'll let it drop.' He looked at Steve as if thinking it might be classified as a lie, but Steve said nothing.'

'Now, what do you know about the murder of Harry Smithson?'

Farrow looked so shocked that for a moment Emily thought that he was going to open the car door and make a run for it.

But then he pulled himself together and said 'I've seen it in the papers, but that's all. You are not trying to say that I had anything to do with it, are you?'

'No, not at all,' she said. 'It's just that we think you may have known some of the people that might have been involved. I am going to mention some names, and you tell me if you know them.'

'Billy Pope.'

'Yes, of course, I know Billy Pope. He's a mad bugger, and so are his two step brothers. Yes, he could murder anyone. But I've not heard anyone say that he might have done it. And I'm not going to ask. The less I see of Billy Pope, the better.'

'Okay, said Emily, what about Arnold Lackford?'

He thought for a moment and then said 'Apart from hearing that he's a millionaire now, I don't know much. He was handy with his fists when he was young and a bit of a sharp operator. But I think he's legit now.'

'What about Ron Tilbrooke?'

'Walter Green and Tilbrooke were thick as thieves when they were young. And they were very good at it. Nick anything and everything, they would in those days. They were a bit older than me, but I thought they were great. I wanted to join them, but they didn't want to know me. I was just a little kid. I used to try and be like them, but nobody wanted to team up with me, and you can't do it properly on your own, and I didn't even have a bike, let alone a car.

'Just when I thought of asking them again because I had grown bigger and stronger by then, suddenly, they went their own ways. I don't think there was a falling out or anything, but within a year or so, Tilbrooke had a good business and Green was living off scraps, like most of us. But that's all I know. Honest, it is.'

'Just one more name,' Emily said, 'Sid Slack.'

'Old Slimy Sid. I don't think he would have the guts to get involved with anything like murder. It got around that he was a police snitch. I have no idea if it was true or not, but from then on, he found it difficult to get work and nobody would tell him anything. People round here don't like that sort of thing. They prefer to sort things out themselves. Last I heard, he was up to his neck in debt.'

'You and Sid seem to have a lot in common,' Steve said

'What do you mean? I would never snitch on anyone,' Farrow said indignantly.

'That's all unless you have anything else to tell us?' Emily asked.

'No, I haven't. Was that alright? I didn't lie once.'

'Congratulations, you've earned a tenner,' said Steve. Farrow held out his hand for the money. 'Just one more thing, if you had to put money on who murdered Harry Smithson, out of the names we have given you, who would you say?'

'That's easy. Billy Pope. He's bloody crazy and can fly into a rage if you look at him the wrong way. But I wouldn't want you to tell anyone that I said that' Farrow said.

'Okay, we are going to drive you home now, and then I will give you the money,' Steve said with a smile.

Farrow, didn't object. He just sat sullenly in the car saying nothing. Steve turned the car around and drove back towards the village. Farrow only became agitated when Steve drove past the muddy road to his house and stopped outside the village shop.

'What are we doing here?' he said.

'We are going in to pay what you owe Mac, and then you can have the rest of the tenner,' Steve said.

'That wasn't the deal,' whined Farrow.

'Mac told us you said that you would come in and pay him when you had the money. And you're a man of your word, aren't you Barry. Carry on like this, and you will become a pillar of the community.'

Steve went into the shop with him and several minutes later emerged smiling. Farrow trudged behind looking miserable.

Steve jumped into the car and Farrow trudged homewards.

'He wanted to walk back. I think he'd had enough of us.' Steve said.

'What a shame, I was hoping that he might ask us in for tea,' Emily said laughingly.

'What he told us confirmed most of what we knew already, and I suppose that is helpful, but it didn't move us forward,' said Steve.

'No, but it was a shot in the dark, and I didn't expect much more.' Emily said. 'I think we'd better go to see Walter Green again tomorrow and really put the pressure on to get a name from him.'

CHAPTER 21

Emily and Steve followed the now established ritual of going into the office, looking at the few items of post that had been left for them and then going to the store office. Today, they did not need to because they had kept everything they needed with them so that they could make a quick start in the morning. They walked to the pool car garage and then drove out on the A47 towards Wisbech.

A steady drizzle had set in overnight, and the fens looked very different from the day, just a few weeks ago, when the sun shone brightly and magnificent white clouds floated by on a gentle breeze.

Now the fens were cold, grey, and mysterious. The misty drizzle reduced visibility to a few car lengths in front of them and the windscreen wipers beat out a monotonous rhythm. The heater in the car seemed not to be working at all and Steve was constantly having to wipe away the mist that was forming inside the windscreen. He did this with an old rag that he found in the pocket of the car, but this was soon saturated and useless.

By the time they reached Thorney, the heater had started to blow a little warm air into the car, and the journey seemed to be improving. But progress was slow, with tractors and trucks making their sedate way across the countryside.

It was nine-thirty in the morning, but it looked like late evening.

'I hate this road in weather like this,' Steve said.

'I'm glad it's not me driving,' Emily replied. She hadn't really noticed what driving conditions were like. Her mind had raced ahead to the meeting with Walter Green. This had to be the day when he told them who it was that he was protecting. But she had been disappointed so many times that she just could not imagine that it was actually going to be resolved today.

'I hope that Walter is ready to be reasonable. You are right that we have to press him, but I would hate anything to happen to him by pushing him too far,' she said to Steve.

'I know what you mean,' he said. 'In many ways, he seems to be a decent sort of bloke. But if he was involved in a crime, that he says himself was terrible, then no matter how long ago it was, those involved should have to answer for it.'

She nodded. 'I know that it has to be done, it's just that I don't know if I can do it.'

'We can do it,' he said. 'We'll do it together, and it will be okay. I think that he really took on board what I said about the danger he had put you in. Maybe now he can see that it has to come out into the open, he will have built up the courage to tell us what happened all those years ago. We have told him several times that once we know the story, we can get protection for him from the police. So let's hope that he is ready to talk.'

When they arrived at Walter's house, they knocked on the door, but no one answered. They walked to the back door and tried again, but still, no one came. They were beginning to get very wet and cold in the persistent drizzle and were just considering going back to the car when Elsie looked round the corner of Walter's house.

'Thank goodness; it's you,' she said. 'I didn't know what to do.'

'Where is Walter? Is he alright? Emily asked.

'I don't know,' Elsie replied. 'Let's get inside. I've got a key.'

She opened the door at the front of the house and led them inside. The room was considerably tidier than usual, so Emily assumed that Elsie had tidied up.

'I went to the shop, as usual, yesterday afternoon and dropped in to see Walter to get his shopping list. He always makes a list for me, so I don't have to remember everything. He seemed to be alright, well as alright as he ever is these days.

'It was when I was on the way back. I was perhaps three hundred yards down the road. Too far to see much, but I noticed a car coming out of our driveway. I couldn't see anyone in it. And it was beginning to get dark, but it definitely came out of this driveway,' she pointed through the window as if to emphasise how sure she was. 'I didn't recognise the car. Well, we hardly get anyone coming to see us by car.'

'And he is definitely not here, in the house or garden?' Steve asked.

Elsie shook her head. 'I called and called, but he didn't answer. Then I went and looked upstairs. There was no one there. Well, no one that I could see.'

'Should I go and look again?' Steve asked.

Elsie nodded. 'If you wouldn't mind. I didn't know what I might find.'

Steve went through to the kitchen and then up the stairs. They could hear his footsteps in the bedroom above.

'So Walter didn't often have visitors?' Emily asked.

'No, almost never and certainly not in a car. The farmer down the road occasionally drops a bag of potatoes off for us, but he just comes in his tractor. The only ones that I can remember recently are you and your friend. I have forgotten his name.'

'Steve,' Emily reminded her.

'Yes, Steve. And of course, there is the doctor who calls from time to time, but I rang him to ask if he had called and taken Walter away, you know, to hospital perhaps. But he said no, he hadn't seen him for several of weeks. He was a bit surprised that Walter would have felt up to going out.'

Steve, returned from his search upstairs and asked if there was anywhere outside where he might have been. Elsie said there was an old shed and a coal house. And at the bottom of the garden, there was an outside toilet that wasn't used anymore. Steve went off to check them out and to look at the garden.

Emily asked Elsie if there was anyone that he talked about, maybe from the old days.

'No, not really. He used to say that in the days when he was near to leaving school and after he left, he used to get into all sorts of scrapes. Mainly with cars, but that often happens around here. There's not enough for young lads to do. Messing about with cars gets a lot of them into trouble at one time or another. Especially if parents don't keep an eye on them.'

'Yes, I can imagine,' said Emily. She couldn't really concentrate on what Elsie was saying. Walter going missing like this was a real blow to their plans and solving the case quickly. It felt as if they were suddenly back to square one. With no real idea of what to do next.

Steve arrived back, looking thoroughly wet and miserable. 'No, he's not out there anywhere, so he must have gone off with someone.'

'And it wasn't the doctor,' Emily said, 'Elsie has already checked with him.'

'We'd better go and let Elsie get on. Don't worry Elsie, when things like this happen there's often quite a simple explanation.'

'Yes, you are probably right, but I won't have you driving all the way back without having a cup of tea and a biscuit with me. Come on I will lock up here, and we'll go next door.'

Emily and Steve exchanged a quick look at each other before accepting Elsie's invitation. What they really wanted and needed to do was to discuss where they go from here, when the man that holds the key to the whole story has suddenly disappeared. But they could not just leave her to worry alone. Emily could imagine that even though Walter was a strange person and had probably been involved in some nasty things in the past, he was all that Elsie had. He was probably what kept her going, knowing that someone depended on her and was giving her life a real purpose.

As there was nothing positive that they could say about Walter's disappearance Emily and Steve deliberately kept off the subject and let Elsie talk about her life. Her house, in stark contrast to Walter's, was immaculately clean and tidy. The tea was good and strong, and her biscuits were homemade and delicious.

She talked about her happy childhood on her father's farm and the tragedy of him being killed in a tractor accident. Then how her mother had to sell the farm and come to live in this house next to Walter. Her mother had died a few years ago, but although Elsie was now on her own, she was still a happy person and was determined to enjoy her life. She proudly showed them her new television that had brought the outside world into her home. She turned it on to show them what it was like, but the picture kept spinning round, and the people on it looked like ghost images. Elsie said it was only like that when the wind was in the wrong direction.

Steve and Emily left the house feeling inspired by Elsie's attitude to life, but even that could not hide the disappointment of Walter's disappearance. There were unspoken questions in both their minds. Would they ever know who Walter's accomplice was in the crime that still haunted him? Would that lead them to the killer of Harry Smithson? Would they ever see Walter Green alive again?

CHAPTER 22

Hunstanton, Norfolk.
October 1961

Peter Jackson rode his bicycle down to the front in Hunstanton. The journey from his smart little bungalow, just a couple of streets away from the seafront, was slightly erratic because of the bucket and spade he had to balance on the handlebars. This was not a sand-castle building bucket and spade; these were his cockling tools.

His journey was short, but he liked to get out on the sands as early as possible. When the tide was out, he was often a lone figure walking across the rippled, wet sand. That was when he was at his happiest. Being first made him feel that he was getting the best cockles. The crème of the crop. The fact that it was obviously potluck, and even the last man on the beach could be the one to get the best cockles; it still didn't shake his belief in striving to be first. The early bird gets the juiciest worm because he deserves it, Peter thought. And consequently, he was always first.

Peter had been a worrier all his life. He had spent most of his time teaching at a primary school on the outskirts of Birmingham, and although he was continually being told by the headmistress that he was doing an excellent job, he somehow felt that he was always letting the children down.

He also convinced himself that he had a chronic chest condition, despite his doctor's reassurance that most people in the country and, particularly those living in big cities, had the same problems as he did. Eventually, his doctor got so fed up with Peter's constant visits to the surgery, that he suggested that he might like to consider early retirement. A move to the coast, where the air was cleaner and the sea breezes more bracing, might do him the world of good the doctor said. To Peter's surprise, he immediately liked the idea, and when he suggested it to his wife Maureen, she also thought that it was a good idea.

After extensive research at the local library, Peter and Maureen decided on Hunstanton, a pleasant little seaside town on the North-West Norfolk coast, where the Wash meets the North Sea. Affectionately known as 'Sunny Hunny' by the locals and the many regular visitors it has every year, it had a pier, a fun fair, a cinema and enough shops to make it self-sufficient for most things.

He and Maureen had set their heart on a sea view, but when it came down to it, they decided to save what was a considerable sum of money, by settling for a property a couple of streets back from the seafront.

From inside the bungalow, the day looked pleasant and sunny for October, but by the time Peter had wobbled his way down to the front, the wind was whipping off the North Sea, and the sky was darkening. He wished that he had put his big topcoat on, rather than his windcheater. He thought about going back, but a quick glance told him he was going to be first on the beach today, and that was something he could not resist. He chained his bike to a seafront lamppost, picked up his bucket and spade and walked down the steps and onto the beach.

This was about the only part of his life in retirement that he really enjoyed. He wanted to be like the local men. People who understood the sea, winds, weather and tides. Men who could go fishing and bring home tonight's dinner. Folk who would look at the sky and sea and tell you it would be raining within the hour.

He would love to learn from them, but the problem was he found it difficult to talk to them. As a teacher of small children, he had been the one with all the knowledge. They asked the questions and he had the answers. Now the local men of Hunstanton had the answers and felt that asking them questions made him feel slightly inadequate. It dented his pride, seeking knowledge from men who had probably had very little education.

The only thing that he had picked up from them was how to go cockling. And that was because he could stand and see what they did from a distance.

The tide was well out beyond the end of the pier, so there was already a good strip of sand just waiting for him to test his skills. His plan was to go out with the tide and when it turned, just walk back to his bike, and go home. He started to look for the tell-tale signs, that experienced cockler's can spot, but he really had no idea what he was looking for.

Peter worked hard, finding cockles, washing the sand off them and filling his bucket with the little shellfish. The irony was that Peter did not like cockles at all. He had only tried to eat one once and had to spit it out. But he loved finding and harvesting them and Maureen loved them. So that made it worthwhile. It made him feel part of the town and Maureen was always appreciative of his catch.

After about an hour, Peter looked back towards the town and realised he had come quite a long way. He turned to see how far the tide was out and that was when he saw the strange black thing lying stranded on the sand. It was some way from him still and he could not quite make out what it was. He picked up his bucket and shovel and walk towards it. It looked as though someone had dumped a load of rubbish in a big black bag.

Peter had heard that the ships coming into port at King's Lynn, Sutton Bridge or Boston often dumped their rubbish in the sea, rather than disposing of it when they reached port. Peter fumed. It was sheer bloody laziness. He would see if he could find something to identify which ship's crew had thrown it overboard.

He was within about twenty yards of the object when he suddenly stopped in his tracks. It was a body. A man's body. He could see the head, the white face and the black hair. He was dressed in a long coat, black trousers, and large black boots.

Peter look desperately around for someone to help him. He could only see one person, and that was a lone figure digging for cockles near the end of the pier. He usually stayed away from other cocklers. The few he had spoken to were not the sort of people he would normally converse with. But now it was different, he needed help, quickly.

He ran as fast as he could, in his wellington boots and carrying a bucket and spade. Now and then he stopped and shouted. But a single voice on a broad expanse of sand, with the wind blowing from the North East, is lost in a second. He was about ten yards from the man and very out of breath before he could make him hear.

The man looked up, alarmed at Peters panic. 'What's the matter mate?' he said.

Peter was gasping for breath and couldn't get a word out. 'Come on, calm down mate and tell me what the problem is.'

'A body,' gasped Peter. 'A man's body. Out there. We've got to get help before the tide comes in.'

'Are you sure he's dead. Might be a swimmer who's taking a rest.'

'He's wearing a big black overcoat and hobnail boots,' shouted Peter irritably.

'Okay, okay, I was just asking. I'll get some of the lads to come and help. They've got a tractor and trailer. And we will ring the police.'

Peter went from panic to euphoria in seconds. 'Thank you very much; I am afraid I panicked a bit.'

'Don't worry about it mate,' he laughed. 'You're not from around here are you?' He was a man in his early twenties, with a cheerful disposition, who looked as if nothing could panic him. What surprised Peter was that he was wearing a t-shirt, jeans rolled up to the knee, with bare feet. He didn't seem to notice the biting wind and how cold the water was.

'No,' Peter said. 'My wife and I came to retire here a few months ago from Birmingham.'

'You have to be ready for anything round here, kids getting lost, people drowning, people getting swept out to sea. But when it happens we all rally round and get it sorted. Of course, sometimes, like your bloke out there,' he nodded seaward, 'there's not much we can do except bring them ashore. But, looking on the bright side, we save plenty of others. I'll go and round up the posse.'

He hurried off as if this was the most exciting thing that had happened for many a month.

Peter stood, gazing around, and wondering if he ought to do something. The young man in the t-shirt seemed to be getting a group of willing helpers together. Another older man was trying to get a little grey tractor started. Several others gathered round the ancient machine, which was liberally covered in patches of rust. Each time they tried to start it, it coughed little clouds of black smoke out of its exhaust pipe. They persisted and on about the tenth go it spluttered into life.

After about twenty minutes a police car arrived, followed by a small black van. Two policemen walked over to the small group that had gathered around the tractor. Peter saw the young man speak to them and then point at him. He gave them a wave of acknowledgement. Then the tractor revved up and moved slowly forward across the sand, followed by the little group of helpers. Being towed behind the tractor was a flatbed trailer. The whole group moved very slowly forward, and with the men following behind, it looked like a funeral procession that had lost the coffin, Peter thought. As they passed Peter, one of the policemen broke away from the group and came over to him.

'Good morning Sir. I understand that you are the man who spotted the body.' The Constable was a large man in all directions, although Peter noticed that he had been wise enough to put on a large overcoat and as a result looked bigger than he probably was. At least he looked comfortably warm in the very bracing conditions.

'Yes, I didn't think it was a body at first. I thought it was a large sack of rubbish that had perhaps been thrown overboard by a ship. But when I got closer, I could see it wasn't.'

'Could I have your name please Sir?'

'Yes, Peter Jackson.'

The Constable went on to ask for Peter's contact details.

'Well,' said the policeman. 'I think that is all I need from you Sir and if there is anything else, we'll be in touch.'

Peter walked back towards the shore, with a slight feeling of anti-climax. But at least he had a good story to tell Maureen when he reached home. In fact, he had had a very good day because when he went to ride home on his bike, the cockles were so heavy he couldn't keep his balance and had to walk, pushing his bike with the bucket of cockles hooked over the handlebars.

CHAPTER 23

October 1961.

Emily and Steve spent the whole weekend getting to know each other. After the happenings of the week, they were both feeling down because of the lack of progress they had made with the Smithson story.

They were still living apart and yet both wanted to be together. If they had been able to get the mystery of the Harry Smithson story told, and weren't so determined to keep their relationship a secret from the newsroom comedians, they could have been seen openly around the town together. As it was, they needed a place where they could go and not be recognised.

Emily broached the subject first. 'I've been thinking,' she said. 'Is there any reason that we shouldn't let it be known that we are a couple? Does it really matter?'

'Well no, not really,' said Steve thoughtfully. 'But with us being out of the office all the time and not being able to make any progress with this story, people might start thinking that we... well, haven't been giving our full attention to getting the job done. We know that's not true, but if we don't get this resolved soon, there will be plenty of accusations flying about. Our job is to get the story. And if we don't we will have some explaining to do. I don't want people saying that we didn't get it done because we were distracted by personal matters.'

Emily nodded. 'Yes, I see what you mean. It would look exactly like that. We need to get the story finished. That is the only way that we can justify the time we have spent on this.'

'Look, what if we get away for the weekend?' Steve said. They were sitting in the storeroom office late on Friday afternoon after they had returned from the unsuccessful trip to see Walter Green.

Emily, who was feeling really down after Walter's disappearance, was immediately attracted to the idea. 'Yes, I'd love to get away for a short break, but where could we go?'

'Well,' Steve said, 'I think Stamford would be too close. Lots of people live there and come to work in Peterborough. What about Cambridge?'

'That would be great,' she said, 'but is it too far on the Lambretta?'

'No, it's only about thirty-five miles or so. It will be fine. We can have a break in Huntingdon if we like. What do you think?'

'Yes, yes,' she said and flung her arms around him. 'It will be wonderful to get away from all this and really get to know each other.'

'Yes, but I was thinking as we drove back here today that I seem to have known you for months, and yet it is only really a few days. I didn't want to spend another weekend away from you, especially knowing that you are only a couple of miles away. I am just pleased that you are happy. Let's go to Cambridge and have some fun.'

'It's crazy but nice. Where are we going to stay?' she asked.

'We will find a hotel. Don't worry. There are dozens of them, and it will be somewhere nice.'

They arranged to meet at nine-o-clock on Crescent Railway Bridge and agreed that clothes would have to be kept to a minimum because of the scooter's limited space for carrying luggage.

Emily had told Viv that she was going home to see her parents. Viv's smile told Emily that she wasn't fooled for a moment. Emily felt bad about not being able to talk to Terry and explain the way she felt, but they had made no arrangements to meet, and it was not unusual for them not to be together over the weekend.

The weekend in Cambridge was just what they needed. They walked around the town and the Backs and talked about each other. The things they liked and the things they don't like. They talked about the past and growing up, and they talked about the future and their ambitions.

When they got back to Peterborough and Steve was dropping Emily off just a little way from her flat, they found it really difficult to say good night. And Emily stood and watched Steve speed away on the Lambretta. She could not turn away until he was completely out of sight.

As Emily walked into the office on Monday morning, she felt wonderfully happy, totally relaxed, and ready for anything the week could throw at her. She was in love.

Steve was on the phone when she reached her desk, and they both exchanged quick, knowing smiles.

He finished his conversation and put the phone down, looking shocked.'

'What is the matter?' asked Emily.

'That was my mate who works on the King's Lynn paper. They have found another body. At Hunstanton this time.'

'Does he know who it is?' she asked, feeling a wave of shock run through her.

'Yes.' Steve said shaking his head in disbelief.

'Not Walter, is it. Surely not,' she said, sitting down and covering her face with her hands.

'No, not Walter. It's Sid Slack. Let's go to the other office and think what to do next,' he whispered to her. They gathered their things and left.

When they arrived at the office, Steve made coffee with the kettle and instant coffee that he had asked Betty to organise for them. He poured the coffee, and they sat and faced one another.

'We have to be very careful now,' Steve said. 'We need to keep what we know to ourselves for the time being, but we have to be ready to get the information to the police as soon as we are able.'

'The question is, how do we achieve that without It going public and half of Fleet Street descending on us?' he said.

'Talk to Mike Townsend,' she suggested. 'It's how I was working before, and he was excellent at understanding the constraints we were working under, and also at telling me about the leeway he had in working with us. If we do it right, we can all come out looking okay.'

Steve nodded. 'I am beginning to think there is no other way. We need an ally inside the police and Townsend is happy to work that way. There are a few things that we know and haven't been sharing with him. We will have to come clean about the instructions from Martin Yates to keep the investigation secret and the difficulties that has created. Call him now and ask him to meet up with us as soon as possible.'

Emily made the call and was put through. She explained that she had a lot to discuss with him and needed to meet urgently. She also told him that she would like him to meet with Steve Moon and that they are now working on the case together. Mike suggested that they meet at the Royal Oak in Castor, a small village not far from Peterborough, at around twelve today. He said they could sit in either of the cars and talk privately. Then have a drink and sandwich in the pub.

She told Steve the arrangements and asked him if he knew where the pub was, as she had never heard of it. They then made a list of all the things they needed to talk about and agreed that they were going to be totally honest about their concerns that they may never know who Walter Green's partner in crime was.

When they arrived in the pub car park, Mike Townsend was already there. His was the bigger car, so Emily and Steve joined him. He was parked in the far corner out of sight of most people visiting the pub.

Emily got into the front passenger seat, and Steve climbed into the rear seat, immediately behind her.

She introduced Steve to Mike Townsend, and they shook hands.

She explained to Mike that it had become difficult for them to keep him fully informed about the progress they had been making because the editor had made such a big point of their work being kept a secret and that his main concern was possible leaks to the national press.

'Yes, I can appreciate that,' he said. 'You put a lot of work in, have committed a lot of resources and you want to get a return.'

'Yes,' said Steve. 'It has made life difficult for us; we are even working away from the newsroom at the moment. But now, with this latest news about the body that was found on the beach at Hunstanton, we think it is time for us to tell you what we know and unfortunately, that means going behind the editors back.'

'I understand that completely,' Townsend said. 'But what you tell me is just between us. If anything is going to be said in public, I will always warn you in advance. And Emily will tell you I am a man of my word.'

'Yes, she already has. That is why we are here now.'

Between them, Emily and Steve told him about their visits to see Ron Tilbrooke, Barry Farrow and Sid Slack. Now that Sid Slack had been identified as the victim at Hunstanton, they needed to tell everything they knew about him and his efforts at blackmailing Walter Green.

'We still think that Billy Pope, should not be ruled out. He seems to be the one with the temperament for these crimes and has the motive, but he also seems to have left the area. Have you had any sightings?' asked Steve.

'No, not a thing,' said Townsend. 'I think after the episode with Emily in the Cathedral precincts, our road blocks and other activities put the wind up him and he must have gone somewhere to lie low.'

'So, we are left with Lackford, Tilbrooke or Green himself,' Emily said. 'It is possible that Green made up all this about an accomplice, just to buy himself some more time.'

'So, is it time for you to go back to Green and put the squeeze on him.' Townsend said.

'We have tried, but Green has gone missing. The elderly lady who lives next door says that she saw a car leaving their driveway and when she got back to her house, Green had gone, without leaving a note,' said Emily. 'She looks after him, and he is very ill indeed, so she can't understand him leaving like that.'

The Inspector thought for a few minutes and then said. 'I'll give Tilbrooke and Lackford a call and tell them that Green has gone missing and that we are looking for him in connection with these murders. I'll say that we are calling everyone we can think of that has had any sort of contact with him in the past. I'll say he could be dangerous and so on. I'll make it sound as if we are not interested in them.'

They all agreed to keep in touch, and Steve and Emily said they were going to meet one of Steve's old colleagues to find out more about Sid Slack's murder. She said that they would ring him from a phone box in Hunstanton, to see if he had managed to talk to Tilbrooke or Lackford.

They said they would have to skip the visit to the pub and get on their way to meet Steve's contact in King's Lynn.

CHAPTER 24

The drive to King's Lynn was uneventful. Steve was now used to the unpredictability of the traffic, slow and almost stopped one minute, then an open road ahead of the next. Emily felt surprisingly relaxed. She still felt happy from the two wonderful days they had spent in Cambridge and the concerns for the next few days had not really registered with her.

They chatted, spasmodically about their next moves and what Mike Townsend might be able to do for them, but there seemed to be no real clarity in how it all might go. She felt that this might be the lull before the storm, but from which direction the storm might come from; she had no idea.

They both agreed that they would be very guarded with Steve's contact, Paul, about how their investigation was going and how Sid Slack fitted into the overall picture. Steve said Paul was a good bloke, but he was also a journalist. He would probably be happy to tell them things that they would soon be able to get elsewhere, but he would also be pumping them for any scraps of information that might give him a better story.

'So, what do we want to know from him?' Emma asked.

'Where the body was found, how was he killed, how long had he been in the water, stuff like that.'

'And what should we tell him?'

'That we met him once, and he tried to sell us a story, but wouldn't tell us what the story was. So, we told him to stuff his story, and that was the last we heard from him. That's almost true.

'Then, to explain our reason for wanting to meet up with Paul, we say we hoped that he might throw some light on what Sid Slack was trying to sell.'

Emily smiled and nodded her head. 'I'm beginning to understand the thought processes of a journalist. The main rule is trust nobody, even another journalist.'

'Especially another journalist,' Steve said with a laugh.

They stopped at the newspaper office in King's Lynn and were told by the receptionist that Paul was still at Hunstanton and would meet them outside the pier amusements.

They continued the journey from King's Lynn along the A149. Emily had never visited this part of the Norfolk coast and was surprised at the beautiful countryside as the road snaked its way through Castle Rising and then to Sandringham, which looked magnificent in it's Autumn colours.

They reached Snettisham, where all this had started, and Steve pointed to the road which led down to the beach where the first body was washed up. They reached Hunstanton at five minutes past two. Sitting comfortably in the car, Emily and Steve looked at the one or two locals who were hurrying about their business, most of them wearing topcoats, scarves, and gloves and leaning forward into the brisk wind, which was blowing in off the sea.

They drove down the small road to the promenade and Steve could see Paul talking to a couple of men who looked like local fishermen and a uniformed policeman. He saw Steve and immediately pulled away from them and ran towards the car. Steve and Emily climbed out of the car and were both hit by the biting wind. They shook hands, and Steve introduced Emily.

Paul shook her hand and suggested they got out of the wind by going to a little café on the front. It's not good, but it's the only one that opens in winter. They went inside and sat at a table near the window.

Paul was about five-foot-nine, Emily estimated, with a stocky build and broad shoulders. He had a ruddy complexion that tended to make him look older than he was.

He ordered three coffees by calling out to a young girl behind the counter. Emily couldn't help but notice that she was making them from a bottle of Camp Coffee Essence. Paul saw her looking and laughed.

'It's still better than the tea, believe me,' he said. 'Sugar and milk for you both. I'd advise it; its takes away the taste of the coffee essence!'

They both said yes, and Paul called to the girl behind the counter. 'Milk and sugar in all three and could you stir them please.' Emily looked at him in surprise.

'The spoon is on a chain,' he explained. Saves us getting up.'

'Well Steve, long time no see. How are things going?'

'Pretty well I think, what about you?'

'You know me, Steve, always think I should be doing better, but too lazy to do anything about it.'

'And what about you Emily? They weren't making journalists that looked like you when I was at college. Where are you from?'

'St Albans,' she said with a smile.

'Welcome to Sunny Hunny. It does look better than this in Summer.'

'I'm sure it does,' she said.

'So, what can you tell us?' Steve said

'I was just going to ask you that?' answered Paul.

Emily said, 'Sid Slack phoned me and said that he had a story to tell and he wanted money for it. Steve and I went to meet him, and he refused to tell us what the story was until we had paid him a large sum of money. Big money, was the way he put it. We tried to persuade him to give us a little insight into what is was about, but he said no, he would go elsewhere. And that was it, but we are naturally curious about what it was.'

'I don't have any information like that, in fact, I know very little at all,' said Paul, 'but I have learnt that he was stabbed. One well-directed wound. His coat pockets were filled with stones and broken bricks in a futile attempt to get the body to sink, and they think he had been in the water for about eighteen hours. But that I am told is just a rough guess at present.'

'How did they identify him so quickly?'

'His wife had reported him missing, about Wednesday or Thursday last week.'

'Who found the body?' asked Emily.

'An old guy is doing a bit of cockling over the weekend.' Paul pulled his notebook out of his pocket and opened it. 'A retired teacher from Birmingham. He lives locally if you want to speak to him.'

'No, I don't think he could tell us anything. I know when people find bodies they often turn out to be the killer, but if the body had been in the Wash for eighteen hours,' Steve said. 'he did well to predict where it would come ashore. What are the local police thinking about the case?'

'They're not very interested at all. They think it's a problem for the coppers around your way. It's just a routine housekeeping job for the local lads. Sorry, I can't tell you more, I was hoping you would have something for me.' Paul said.

'No, not yet, but we live in hope. I'll keep you posted.'

They stood up to leave, and Paul went over to pay the girl for the coffees.

'Let me get those Paul, you were doing us a favour,' said Steve.

'You deserve a medal for drinking it; this is the least I could do.' The girl behind the counter smiled as if Paul had just complimented her.

They drove the car up into the back streets of Hunstanton and found a telephone box. Emily got out of the car and called Mike Townsend. He told her he had tried ringing Tilbrooke and Lackford, but neither of them were there. He said he was calling tomorrow morning again.

CHAPTER 25

The following morning Emily woke early, which was unusual because normally Viv had to tap on the wall and shout 'it's eight-o-clock'. It was an arrangement they had since the day after Emily moved in. On the first day, Viv had gone off to work, and Emily had slept until nine. Fortunately, she hadn't started the job, but it was either buy an alarm or rely on Viv.

She had a feeling of excitement or, maybe anticipation, inside her, a bit like when she was going somewhere new on holiday. But she couldn't understand why because the prospects of the day being in any way exciting were not good. They seemed to be going round in circles, talking to the same people day after day and getting nowhere.

She knew that Steve would say that is just the nature of a journalist's life. Just enjoy the highs when they come, because there will be plenty of lows as well. But she also knew that Steve was as concerned as she was that the whole thing could go wrong for them. They might never find out who Walter's accomplice was. Walter could well be dead. Equally, some other journalist from another newspaper might stumble across the story and get the breaks that she and Steve so badly needed.

She got up, showered and was sitting drinking a coffee when Viv got up.

'What are you doing up at this time?' Viv asked.

Emily shrugged her shoulders. 'I woke up early and just couldn't sleep. I don't know why. Just one of those things.'

'Everything okay with you and Steve?'

Emily just nodded and smiled. She felt she ought to say more, but she just couldn't start to describe how she felt about him. She had never felt this way before and, strangely, it was quite frightening.

'As well as that? I can read the signs Emily, and I am so pleased for you.'

'I really must talk to Terry; I have treated him really badly.'

'Don't worry. I have been doing the diplomatic bit, breaking the news to him a bit at a time.' Viv said.

'And is he OK about it?' Emily asked.

'He's getting over it. Do you still have feelings for him?'

Emily thought for a few moments and then said, 'Well yes, I really did like him, but at the same time it felt that long term it wasn't going to work. You know how it is.'

'I'm glad you said that because Terry and me have been... well seeing each other. He kept coming round to find out about you, and after a while, we sort of gelled.'

Emily went over to Viv and gave her a hug. 'I am so pleased; I know I have been rotten to him and he didn't deserve that.'

'Don't worry. Terry and me get along great, his shyness and my noisiness go well together. He's only a couple of years younger than me, and he's got a car! It's a romance made in heaven,' Viv laughed.

Emily arrived at work in the best of spirits. The situation with Terry had been weighing on her mind, but with work, and falling in love with Steve, there seemed to be no time to talk to Terry. And Viv deserved someone like Terry, rather than the waster she used to live with.

Steve looked over to her and spoke quietly. 'In the absence of anything else to do I think we'd better go and see Elsie, just in case Walter has returned. We can't sit around waiting for things to happen.'

'Okay, and she might have something more to tell.'

'I have already collected the pool car, it's parked outside.'

'Let's go then,' she said.

The wind had dropped from yesterday, and it looked almost like summer again, except for the piles of leaves that were covering the grass verges. Once passed Thorney there were no trees lining the road, so there were no piles of leaves. The low sunshine was behind them, and the road ahead was clear.

Emily told Steve about Terry and Viv, and he was really pleased for them.

'That's brilliant news,' he said. 'I didn't know how you were going to tell Terry, or how he might take it. Do you think they will make a good couple?'

'Yes, I do,' said Emily. 'With his calm common sense and her extrovert character, I think they will get along well.'

They arrived at Elsie's house at just before ten. Walter's cottage still looked empty, and Elsie opened the door to greet them.

'Have you heard anything about Walter?' she asked as soon as they got out of the car.

'No,' said Emily, 'we hoped that he might have come home.'

'No, there is no sign of him, and I am getting really worried. He was ill. He should be here, in his own home. That's how he wanted to die,' she said, a tear running down her cheek.

They went into Elsie's house, and she said that she would make a cup of tea for them.

'So, you have heard nothing from anyone,' Elsie said as she carried the tray of teacups in from the kitchen and began to pour the tea.

'No, nothing, but we are going to call the police in a short time. They were going to call a couple of people who might know the whereabouts of Walter.'

'I think I'll do it now, we need to do something' said Emily. 'Could we use your phone?'

'Yes, of course,' she replied, 'it's over there. The phone stood on a small round table, next to the fireplace.

Emily asked for Mike Townsend, and after she had told them her name, she was put straight through.

He quickly answered. 'Hello Emily,' he said. 'I'm glad you called early. Where are you.'

'Steve and I are with Elsie, Walter's neighbour. She's very worried about him.'

'I spoke to Ron Tilbrooke a few minutes ago, and he says that Walter is okay but very ill. He said that he had heard he was ill and decided to go and see him to see if he could help. He said that Walter looked so bad he decided to take him back to his house and look after him there.'

'Well at least he is being looked after,' Emily said.

'And to be extra sure,' said Mike Townsend, 'I called the local police in March and asked them to get round there to see if he ought to be taken to the hospital. They are on their way now.'

'That is really good. If you have any further news, you can ring us on Elsie's number. She is anxious to know how he is.' Emily gave him the number and rang off.

Emily gave them a condensed version of what Mike Townsend had told her.

'I just don't understand why they didn't leave me a note. Walter knows how I worry about him,' Elsie said.

'If Walter was really ill he maybe didn't think to tell Tilbrooke that you would be worried,' Steve said. 'We will know more after the local police have been round.'

CHAPTER 26

They sat and listened while Elsie reminisced about what a good neighbour Walter had been. Before he was diagnosed with TB, he had done all sorts of odd jobs for her and also looked after her garden. She said he would bike down to the shops for her and give her vegetables off his smallholding. He also redecorated her house and wouldn't take any money from her.

'There was a lot more to Walter than most people thought,' she said. 'He had very little education and yet he was a great reader of anything he could lay his hands on. Newspapers, magazines and books. He told me recently that he would have liked to have been a writer, like you.

'He was interested in many things, but after he was diagnosed, he went downhill fast and seemed to have lost the will to live.'

Now, she had to go to the shops for him and cook most of his meals. She was glad to help him, but he would seldom go to the doctors or bother with the medication they gave him. She said she was happy to do all this because he had been so good to her, but she was worried that he had given up trying to fight the disease.

The telephone interrupted her story. Elsie answered it and then handed the phone to Emily. It was Mike Townsend.

'Emily,' he said, 'the local police have just called. Tilbrooke was not at home when they arrived. They waited for a while but then took the decision to break in. Inside there was no sign of Tilbrooke, but they found Green, and he was dead.

'Oh, my God,' said Emily. 'I can't believe it. I was afraid this might happen, but hoped I was wrong.'

'I am sending some of our officers over to help. I'll be in touch.'

Emily put the phone down and stood there in shock for a minute. Words would not come.

Steve said, 'What's the matter? What did he say?'

'When the local police arrived, nobody answered the door. They waited a while to see if he would return quickly and when he didn't, they broke in. There was no sign of Tilbrooke,' she turned towards Elsie, 'and I am sorry Elsie, but they found Walter, and he had passed away.'

Elsie took the news quietly, without showing emotion. Emily guessed that she really knew that Walter had to be dead. Otherwise he would have made every effort to let her know where he was.

'I knew really,' Elsie said. 'I knew that after he had been away so long that the inevitable must have happened. I am pleased really. I'm sure he wasn't enjoying life anymore. And at last, I can be truthful with you Emily. I hated lying to you, but Walter swore me to secrecy, and I just couldn't let him down. He trusted me.'

'Lying to me about what?' Emily asked.

'His confession, well he called it his life-story, but I think he was joking. The first time he met you, he felt bad about not telling you about what had happened all those years ago. He thought that if he had told you, your life could be in danger; as it turned out you were in danger anyway.

'He started writing it down a few years ago, but when he became ill, he stopped. Then, when you came on the scene, he decided that he would finish it. He asked if I would give it to you when he died and not before. He gave it to me in a sealed envelope.'

'Where is it now?' Emily asked.

'In this drawer here,' she said, searching around in a lower draw for a key and then unlocking the top draw and taking the envelope out. It was written on foolscap lined paper and held together with a paper clip.

As she handed it over Elsie said, 'I had to get the envelope for him from the village shop.'

Emily opened the envelope and drew out the pages. There looked to be around five pages of very clear, but almost childlike writing.

Emily quickly scanned the first couple of pages and then turned to Steve. 'It was Ron Tilbrooke,' she said quickly to Steve.

'Tilbrooke!' Steve said, shaking his head in disbelief. 'What an act that was. He certainly took me in. So, what do we do now?' He was obviously quickly running through the implications of Tilbrooke being the killer. Suddenly, Steve's face changed to one of shock and realisation.

'My God, he's coming here! I thought it was strange that he was not there when the local police arrived,' Steve said. 'Even if they got there and Walter was dead, he could have just said he had just died of natural causes. After all, he had been looking after him for several days, and now he had died. The police would have thought that was to be expected with the advanced stages of TB.

'But he wasn't there. Why, because he needed to be somewhere else and he needed to be there quickly.'

'Why did he need to come here?' Emily asked.

'Because before he died, he got Walter to tell him about his written confession. He must have forced it out of Walter; he would never have told him willingly. But it can't be difficult to get an old, dying man to tell a secret.

'We have got to move quickly,' Steve said. 'Tilbrooke is almost certainly on his way, and we could be in trouble if we don't get prepared. Fortunately, he won't know that you and I are here,' he said to Emily. 'Let's get that confession well and truly hidden, just in case the worst happens.'

'Emily can you ring Townsend and tell him what's going on. Ask him if he can get the police from Wisbech, or somewhere nearby, to come out to us. In the meantime Elsie, we need to barricade the doors and windows to stop him getting in. Can you go and lock the front and back doors. I am going to move some of the furniture in front of them and the windows.'

Emily called Mike Townsend. As soon as he came on the line, she said, 'It was Tilbrooke. We've got a complete confession. Chapter and verse. The whole story, written by Green himself and left with his neighbour to be passed to me after he died.'

'Thank goodness for that, at last.'

'But Steve thinks we are in real danger now,' she said.

'My God yes, he's right. You have to take steps to protect yourselves, and quickly. We don't know when he left his house.'

'We are barricading the doors and windows and hiding the confession.'

'Good. I'll get onto the local police and get them there as quickly as they can. But it will take a while.'

'We'll do the best we can,' Emily said.

'He's a dangerous and desperate man. He will do everything he can to destroy that confession. He has already killed two or three people; we don't want anymore. Can you get out of the house and hide somewhere?'

'No,' Emily said, 'there are just ploughed fields all around us, and you can see for miles. There is no cover at all. And Elsie is an elderly lady; she won't be able to run across fields. Steve has started building some make-shift barricades to keep him out.'

'Okay, we have already called the police at Wisbech, and so they will be on the way very soon. And I'm coming to you as well. Arm yourself with something that will keep him away from you, like a garden fork.'

Emily put the phone down and went to help Steve in the kitchen. He had made good progress blocking the doors, but the windows were more difficult.

'Where's Elsie,' Emily asked.

'She upstairs looking out for a car approaching. She blames herself for all this, but she wasn't to know how it would work out.'

'Mike says we should arm ourselves with something that we can use to keep him away from us. Like a garden fork.'

'Yes, that's a good idea, but they are outside in the shed. I've gone too far with the barricade now to go outside. We will have to improvise with stuff from in here.'

'Are you scared?' Emily asked Steve.

'Yes, of course, I am. I'm scared for you, and I'm scared for me. I've always been a fighter, not with fists and knives. With words, that's all. I can honestly say I have never had a physical fight in my life. And if we are smart we can think our way through this one as well.'

Emily was getting to know Steve well, and she could tell that he had a plan.

'What are you thinking?' she asked.

'Barricade everything we can, but leave one small weakness, that is big enough for him to get through, but only with difficulty. You and I will be standing by with whatever we can find as weapons and then, as he makes his big entrance, we hit him with all we've got until he's either unconscious or overpowered.'

Just having a plan, no matter how effective it might be, was enough to make Emily feel better. She was ready for the fight now, and they were going to win.

They completed their preparations, and the cottage was as secure as they could make it, except for one small window at the back of the house which had obviously been added recently, to bring extra light into the kitchen. Steve showed Emily that to get through you would have to break the glass, drag yourself through the small window frame, and then across the taps and sink, all of which would take a considerable time and effort. The plan would then depend on whether Emily and Steve had the stomach for beating the hell out of another human being, which at that moment in time they did.

'The best thing about the plan is that he doesn't know who is in here with Elsie,' Steve said. 'It could be anyone, and he doesn't have time to find out. He has got to go for it almost as soon as he gets here. That means he can't do too much thinking and that will be our main advantage.'

A shout came from Elsie upstairs. They ran up to where she was sitting in the front bedroom. They looked out, and there was a truck, parked at the end of the drive. It was one of those all-purpose vehicles that Emily had seen in movies, half truck, half car. The sort that modern-day cowboys like to drive.

'Why has he stopped?' Emily asked.

'Because he doesn't know who our car belongs to. He's weighing up whether to come down or not,' said Steve. 'It's good to put some uncertainty in his mind. I think he will still come; he can't afford not to'

'Elsie, you know that things may get broken when we are trying to stop him getting in, don't you?' he said.

'Don't worry about that she said. I don't mind how you stop him. He is a wicked man and you two are very brave.'

Eventually, the truck began to move slowly down the driveway. The three of them watched the truck slowly draw up alongside their car. Tilbrooke, stepped out of the truck, he was carrying a shotgun, low on his right-hand side, the barrel facing the floor. It looked even more like a scene from an American movie.

He walked cautiously up to Walter's front window and looked in. Then he moved to Elsie's front door and suddenly looked up at the bedroom window. Instinctively, they drew back into the room, but the front of the house was in shadow, so there was little danger of being seen. Elsie walked round her bed and sat on a chair, as far from the window as she could.

Suddenly, there was a loud bang and a sound of shattering glass. Tilbrooke had shot the front window in.

'That was just bravado, making himself feel powerful, but a completely useless gesture. Time to get down there,' said Steve to Emily. He sounded very confident, but Emily knew how be must be feeling.

They moved quickly down the stairs and picked up the weapons they had chosen. Emily had picked a solid, heavy fire poker and Steve a solid wooden chair. From the kitchen, they couldn't see Tilbrooke, but they could hear him walking around. Steve hoped he would notice the weak point in their barricade. The smaller window at the back, where they had just propped a piece of plywood, with an inviting gap through which the kitchen could be seen.

The sound of his feet shuffling around in the back garden seemed to be coming from the window, so far so good. The plan seemed to be working. The next second the room exploded into noise as the butt of the shotgun shattered the glass in the window. Emily and Steve immediately climbed onto their positions. Steve was standing on top of the washing machine, and Emily had one foot on the draining board and one foot on a short piece of worktop. They were both holding their weapons at the ready.

Tilbrooke was using the butt of the gun to clear away and glass left in the frame. Then, with a single lunge, he propelled himself through the window frame. It was an impressive first move. His head was well passed the sink, and his upper body was inside the window. He had landed further into the kitchen than Steve had planned for and he guessed that the shuffling outside the window was Tilbrooke putting a box or something that he could launch himself from.

Steve knew he had to act straight away and slammed the chair down onto Tilbrooke's back. He let out a yell and twisted to see where it came from. The first blow had shattered the chair, but Steve was left with the chair back in his hand, so he hit him again. The back was not very heavy, but it allowed Steve to bring it down quickly and he aimed at Tilbrooke's upper body and head. It caught Tilbrooke on the side of his face and ear and brought more cursing and wailing from him. Blood was coming from a cut on his head, but he still seemed to have plenty of fight left in him.

Steve tried another way. He jumped onto Tilbrooke's back in the hope that the taps he was laying across would do some damage and quieten him down. Instead, it seemed to enrage him more. He reached back into his jacket pocket and pulled something from it. Emily immediately saw that it was a knife. He flicked open the long blade, and at that moment Emily knew she had to react.

She felt the fear welling up inside her, but it was mixed with anger. That knife had already killed at least two men, and now it was Steve who was being threatened. At that moment Tilbrooke tried to lift himself up and throw Steve off his back.

She waited her moment until his right hand was clutching the edge of the sink. The handle of the knife was between the sink and his hand. In an instant, Emily smashed the poker down across his hand with the sort of power she would have put into hitting a hockey ball. There was a cracking sound as the poker hit is mark and a howl from Tilbrooke. She noticed that even with all the screaming, he was still holding the knife loosely in his damaged fingers. She hit him again higher up on his wrist. The knife clattered across the floor. Suddenly the fight seemed to have gone out of him. He looked bewildered and turned to look at Emily who was still standing with the poker in her hand. She lifted it threateningly, but he turned away.

'Fucking interfering bastards,' he whimpered and continued to whine like an injured dog.

Steve got down from the washing machine and took an old cloth and carefully picked up the knife. He laid it out of the way. Emily climbed down as well and stood next to Steve.

'What do we do now?' she asked.

'Get me down from here,' Tilbrook said. 'You've broken my hand and my wrist and some ribs on the bloody taps when you jumped on me.'

'Life's full of disappointments,' Steve said. 'You're staying where you are until the police get here. They shouldn't be long now.' They stood either side of him, Steve had the poker now, and Emily had one leg of the chair, which was about all that was left intact. She had a few practice swings with it, just to deter Tilbrooke from trying to make a comeback.

He made an effort to raise himself from the sink, but Emily lifted the chair leg and said. 'Don't even try to move.'

'I'm in real pain,' he complained, but neither Steve or Emily bothered to answer. In fact, they were both feeling exhausted. The adrenalin rush had gone.

It was another ten minutes before the local police arrived, but it seemed like ten hours. Steve let them in the back door and left them to get Tilbrooke from his place on the sink. Soon afterwards they were followed by DCI Mike Townsend and two of his team.

Outside a circle of flashing blue lights made a dramatic sight across the fenlands. Inside, Steve was relating to Townsend what had happened. Emily was sitting slumped in a chair, feeling as if she had just completed a marathon.

An ambulance was called to take Tilbrooke away, accompanied by two Constables. Mike was organising the other police and said a forensic team was coming over.

When that was all done, he turned to Steve and Emily.

'I'm sorry that you were put in the firing line like that, but sometimes in happens. A case goes on and on with nothing happening, and then everything goes off at the same time. I'm sure that was very frightening, and I bet you are totally exhausted, but you both did a great job.'

'Yes, it was a bit hairy. I don't think either of us want to go through that again,' Steve said.

He showed Townsend where the knife was and how Emily had stopped him from using it. Mike called one of the local officers over to bag it and kept it safe.

'Is there anywhere we can talk and look at that confession?' he asked

'Let's go upstairs, and we can introduce you to Elsie. What's left of this is her house,' Steve said.

Elsie was sitting in her room looking shell shocked. Emily thought that it must have been terrible upstairs, hearing the noise from below and not knowing what was happening.

'I'm so pleased that you and Steve are alright,' she said. 'It sounded terrible. Has that wicked man gone?'

'Yes, we have taken him away,' said Mike.

He said that they would arrange for the house to be made safe. 'It would be a good idea if you could spend a couple of nights away from here. While it gets repaired and tidied up,' he said to Elsie. 'Is there anywhere you could go?

'Yes, I am sure my friend in the village will let me stay with her.'

'Get the things that you will need together and when you are ready I'll get someone to take you there,' Mike said.

'Elsie, I will come over to see you next week, just to make sure you are okay,' Emily said.

'I'll look forward to that Emily. Then you can tell me what was happening downstairs.'

They asked her if it would be alright if they used the back bedroom to have a short meeting, just Mike, Emily and Steve.

She said it was not very comfortable in there, but they were welcome to use it. The three of them crowded into the small room, which had an old lounge chair, a washing basket, and a card table, with two folding chairs.

Emily handed Mike the large envelope, which they had hidden under a rug during Tilbrooke's attempted entry. He looked inside and saw the pages of lined foolscap and asked Emily if she had touched the pages. She said that she did touch the top two when she first looked at it to get Tilbrooke's name. As soon as she saw what it was, she was very careful only to hold the edges and not touch any more than she had to.

'That's okay. We will just need your fingerprints so we can identify them against any others that are there,' he said. He then took some thin gloves out of his pocket and pulled out the pages. He began to read the first page, he scanned through the second page and then stopped.

'Yes, I can see this is very detailed and conclusive. The problem is we both need it now.'

Steve said, 'We can fix that easily. I have a camera in the car that is ideal for this sort of thing. I'll get it, and you put the pages on the card table, and I'll photograph them all. It won't take us ten minutes. Then you have the evidence, and we have the story.'

'That's fine, but don't forget that you won't be able to use most of it until after the trial.'

'No, we won't publish anything that is likely to get the paper into trouble, but just having it on hand now means that we can always be one step ahead later on.'

Steve fetched the camera, and the shots were taken. Elsie left to go to her friends, and some more of Townsend's team arrived. It was late afternoon now, and the light was just beginning to fade. Steve and Emily felt they were getting in the way now, so they agreed with Mike that they would drop in and give him statements in the morning. They could also agree on timings of police statements to the press and publishing the story.

They stopped at the village of Thorney Toll, which was on the main road back to Peterborough. There was a telephone kiosk next to the garage. Steve called Martin Yates and reported that they had everything they needed now and they were on their way back to write the story. He said he would be waiting for them in his office.

Emily then rang Pete and ask him if he could stay a bit later tonight because they had some film to develop and some prints to be made. She said it was about the Harry Smithson story, and impressed upon him that it was secret. He said he was happy to wait and he would tell no one.

Back at the office, almost everyone had gone home when they arrived. They dropped the film off with Pete and then went to see Martin Yates in his office. Steve had told Emily that Martin was a good guy and had stuck his neck out with senior management to keep them on the story, especially following the incident with Arnold Lackford.

Emily was a little worried that he might still be unhappy about her calling Lackford, but the grin on his face when they walked into his office was something to be seen.

'Well done you two,' he said. 'Thank goodness you pulled it off. Otherwise, I would be down at the Labour Exchange tomorrow morning. Tell me, how did it suddenly come to a head like that?'

They gave him a brief rundown of the happenings of the day. Including the confession that had been left with Elsie and the battle with Ron Tilbrooke.

That prompted him to open his cupboard door and produce a bottle of Scotch. He set three glasses on the table and tipped a good measure into each.

'Well, he said holding his glass out towards them. Here's to the dynamic duo. I should think you can do with this after all you have been through. Of course, I should be saying that you should never put yourself in danger like that, but it seems you had very little choice in the matter. But well done, you deserve all the praise that is undoubtedly coming your way.'

'And getting quickly back to business,' he said with a smile. 'What is the plan now, when can we run the story?'

'Emily and I are going to write the first story tonight, and you will have it on your desk first thing in the morning. I'll seal it and mark it only to be opened by you. That should stop any marauding stringers from getting a look at it.'

'Better still,' said Martin, 'put it in the cupboard where the whisky is, lock it and put the key inside this matchbox at the bottom of my desk drawer. And yes, I am paranoid. I have had so many stories nicked from under my nose it's not surprising that I get a bit jumpy about leaks.'

'And there will be plenty of other spin-offs from this, right through to when it comes to trial and probably afterwards,' said Steve.

'And what about this confession?' Yates asked.

'The original is with the police because it is evidence. We have a copy, which Pete is processing now and we will go and collect the prints in an hour. And, before you ask, Pete has been sworn to secrecy.'

'I'm not worried about Pete; he hates telling anyone anything. Even the things he is supposed to tell you.'

'In the morning Emily and I have to go to see Detective Chief Inspector Mike Townsend and give him our statements about what happened today. He's agreed to hold his press conference about the arrest until just after the paper hits the streets. That way no one's going to beat us on this.'

'I won't ask how you managed to wangle that.'

'It's all above board. Emily had already got a good working relationship with him when I joined her on the story. He believes in cooperation with the press, as long as it's two way.'

'Well it certainly worked on this one,' he said, standing up and taking his coat from the back of the door. You might as well work in here tonight; it's warmer than anywhere else. And when this is all over, I am taking you out for a damn good meal. You can even bring girlfriend and boyfriend if you want,' he paused for them to answer and then walked out the door chuckling to himself.

'Do you think he guessed?' asked Emily

'Probably not until he saw the look on our faces, but I think that has let the cat out of the bag. But what does it matter now? Our mission has been achieved, and no one can say that we had it easy.'

CHAPTER 27

The confession

Fortified by Martin's whisky, and some sandwiches that Steve scrounged from the small canteen next to the printing presses, Emily and Steve sat down at the table next to Martin's desk to read Walter's shakily written confession.

Ron Tilbrooke and me had been mates at school. We weren't good at school work and were often in trouble. Ron was always the hard kid of the school. I was the quiet sort and having a gammy leg meant that I got picked on a lot. I decided that keeping on the right side of Ron would save me a lot of bother with the other kids. Nobody bullied me, Ron saw to that.

Then when we got near to leaving school, we didn't bother to go very much. I think the school were glad. We spent our time pinching cars and then driving round look for things to nick and then sell. We were earning a decent living too, but the coppers eventually made it too hot for us, and we decided to think of something else.

Then Ron came to me one day and said someone had told him about this old chap. He was supposed to have a fortune stashed under his bed because he didn't trust banks. We didn't really believe it because in the fens you hear that sort of talk all the time.

But Ron said we might as well go and take a look. What had we got to lose? We drove over for a couple of nights and checked that he did not seem to have any visitors. The house was big, in the middle of nowhere and it looked almost deserted. It almost looked like it was empty, no lights, no smoke from the chimney, no sign of life. We decided to go the next night and see what we could find.

Ron said we should go through the back way so that we weren't seen from the road. We parked the car about a hundred yards away in a layby and walked back. The back door was rotting and gave way at our first push. Inside it was a complete mess, piles of rubbish on the floor – newspapers, tin cans, bottles the lot. The place stunk.

We moved towards the rest of the house, and it was a bit better there. We opened the living room door, and there was the old man, snoring away in an old arm chair. I was ready to run, but Ron, cool as you like, took a flick knife from his pocket. He held it in front of his face and then prodded him awake.

I couldn't believe what I was seeing; I never thought Ron would do anything like this. I told him to stop, but he told me to shut up. He asked the old man where his money was and when he refused to tell him he said he was going to start cuttings bits off him, starting with a finger. I begged him to stop. He told me to go back to the car and bring it back here and park it down the side of the house.

I knew I couldn't stop him, so I went and fetched the car. I backed it right in as far as it would go so it couldn't be seen from the road. I sat and waited for about an hour before Ron came out carrying an old sack. He opened the boot and threw it in and told me to take it steady driving home. I asked him if he had got any money and he said a bit and some other stuff.

When we got to my place, he dropped me off and said he would count it up and share it out tomorrow. To be honest, I didn't really want anything, I wanted to have nothing to do with it, but it was too late for that. He came round the following day and gave me a hundred quid, which was good money in 1936, but as time went by I knew it must have been a lot more than that.

That picture of the old man waking up and Ron waving the knife in front of his face has haunted me ever since. Day and night, it has always been on my mind.

The papers and radio had reported a lot of stuff about the murder of the old man and I was certain that at any time the coppers would be round to my house. Ron said that to keep ourselves safe; we should not be seen together anymore. And we never were. He lived his life, and I lived mine.

I could contact him if I was ever in trouble or needed money and he always looked after me when I did have problems, but it was always in secret. The trouble was that I missed him. I hated what he had done, but I was lost without him. I had lost my prop in life, and from then onwards I just existed. It was my punishment, and it was all I deserved.

I felt so miserable that a couple of years later I was in a pub and there was a young guy there, who I knew vaguely, so we started to chat and drink. It was Harry Smithson, and he was telling me about his ambitions to become a boxer. He was a real nice lad, down to earth and he opened his heart to me about how he hoped to make it big but didn't really know if he was good enough.

He was so honest with me, I felt that I could be honest with him and told him what had happened that night with the old man. I said how it haunted me now and in our drunken stupor, we tried to make each other feel better.

Next day, when I sobered up, I felt that I had let Ron down, so I called him and told him what had happened. He was really pissed off with me and still is. He said he would take care of it and he later told me that he had tried to track Smithson down, but he had been called-up and gone off to the war.

Ron managed to avoid the war with a perforated ear drum, and I had my gammy leg. I thought nothing more about Harry Smithson until I read in the paper about the body in the Wash and how no one had been able to identify it. I knew that Ron liked to go fishing and had a boat moored at Long

Sutton. Then it came out that the body was Smithson and I knew Ron was behind it.

When Sid Slack came trying to blackmail me, with his story about overhearing Harry and me in the pub, I couldn't believe this was happening after all these years. I felt sure there was no one else in the bar when Harry and me were talking. The landlord of the pub had gone out the back to change a barrel, and he was gone a long time. But there could have been someone else there. I was so pissed I wouldn't have noticed.

I gave him all the money I had and promised more. When I called Ron and told him, I knew what the outcome would be. But what could I do?

I haven't written this because I want anyone to feel sorry for me. It was all my own fault, and the way my life turned out was what I deserved. I just want Ron to answer for his part in this terrible crime because I have never heard one word of regret from him.

It was signed and dated.

'Well, what a way to mess up a life,' said Steve.

'You can't help but feel a bit sorry for Walter, but he did bring it on himself,' said Emily. 'And Ron Tilbrooke could turn on the charm when he wanted too. Even with everything pointing at him and, after our visit to him, I still had my doubts that he was the killer.'

'Once that first murder had been committed, the damage had been done,' said Steve.'

'Yes,' said Emily, 'that led to Tilbrooke having to kill Harry Smithson and then to having to silence Sid Slack. Each murder was the inevitable consequence of the others.'

'And I don't think it stopped there,' Steve said. 'I think we will find that although Walter was dying, in trying to get him to admit to writing his confession and telling him where it was, probably hastened the end for him.

'Yes,' agreed Emily. 'I guess you have to have a sort of split personality to be like that. It is difficult to imagine people being able to put horrendous things they have done completely out of their mind and just get on with life as if nothing had happened. It was something Walter couldn't do and, in the end, it brought them both down.

'Let's get this written,' Steve said. 'I don't know about you, but I've had enough for one day.'

They typed the story, read it a couple of times, and then put it back in Martin's cupboard, together with the whisky. Emily locked the cupboard and put the key in the drawer.

They looked at each other and Emily said, 'Are you thinking the same thing that I am thinking.'

'I don't know,' Steve laughed. 'You tell me what you're thinking first.'

'I am absolutely exhausted, but I don't want to go home. Not on my own. I want to be with you.'

'Yes, wouldn't that be great. When you've gone through something like that you need to be together,' he said.

'But we can't go to Viv's. Terry might be there, and I don't want to face him tonight, even though I know it is alright. And I know what it's like at Viv's. It's far too cosy. It would be embarrassing.'

'If we were very quiet we could go to my place. The landlady lives upstairs, and she is the old-fashioned sort. I'm not supposed to have 'visitors' staying overnight. But why not risk it for one night. It's time we got a place of our own anyway, so what does it matter if she throws me out.'

The End

About the author

After a lifetime of working in PR and Market Communications, writing brochure copy, advertisements, video scripts and web copy to help sell other peoples' products, I reached retirement and came to the inevitable question, 'What to do next?'

My wife and I enjoy travelling, particularly in Europe, and we also love jazz, photography and watching cricket and football.

But even with all that, there seemed something missing. We are both avid readers and during my younger years I wrote short stories for magazines. The idea to start writing a novel came out of the blue and now it is an important part of our lives.

I have lived all my life in and around Peterborough and love the fens and North Norfolk coast, so inevitably it is where my first book is set.

Ian D Wright

Printed in Great Britain
by Amazon